presents

CELEBRATING

INDIA

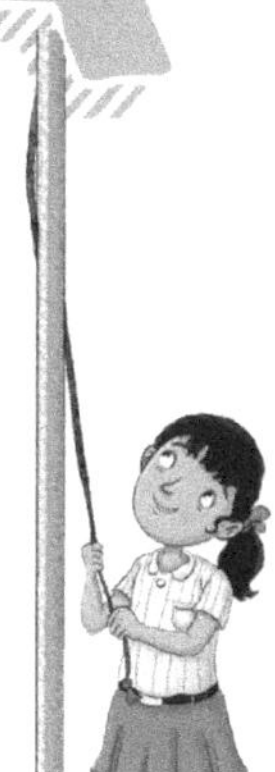

RUPA

Published by
Rupa Publications India Pvt. Ltd 2022
7/16, Ansari Road, Daryaganj
New Delhi 110002

Sales Centres:
Allahabad Bengaluru Chennai
Hyderabad Jaipur Kathmandu
Kolkata Mumbai

ISBN: 978-93-5520-842-2

First impression 2022

10 9 8 7 6 5 4 3 2 1

Printed in India

Freedom, Independence and Democracy

From Mohandas to Mahatma

The Struggle

A Pledge

Freedom, Independence and Democracy

UNFOLD THE MAGIC OF THESE SPECIAL WORDS

Flag Day

In this Independence Day parade, find 4 Indian flags, a boy with cap, a mic, a piece of paper and 3 green balloons.

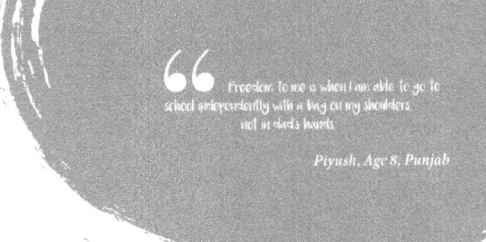

Aazaadi
The Meaning of Freedom

By Poonam Mehta

Chirag was excited today. He was neatly dressed in his school uniform and had pinned his house badge to his chest. He had been selected for the school **parade** and was going to lead his house. The house that marched the best would get a prize.

Preparations for the parade had been taking place for a while now. Every morning, students would begin practicing immediately after the school prayer. They would march around the school ground and day by day, they got better. The kids were also practicing skits, folk dances and PATRIOTIC songs. They were getting ready for the Independence Day celebrations at school. India was celebrating its 75TH year of independence this year.

Because he was leading his house, Chirag needed to look perfect. For this he needed to keep his shoes shiny, his uniform needed to be CLEAN and ironed and his hair and nails needed his attention too. All the effort he put in to this made him disciplined. He automatically started faring better in his tests and was even getting an award for having 100% attendance.

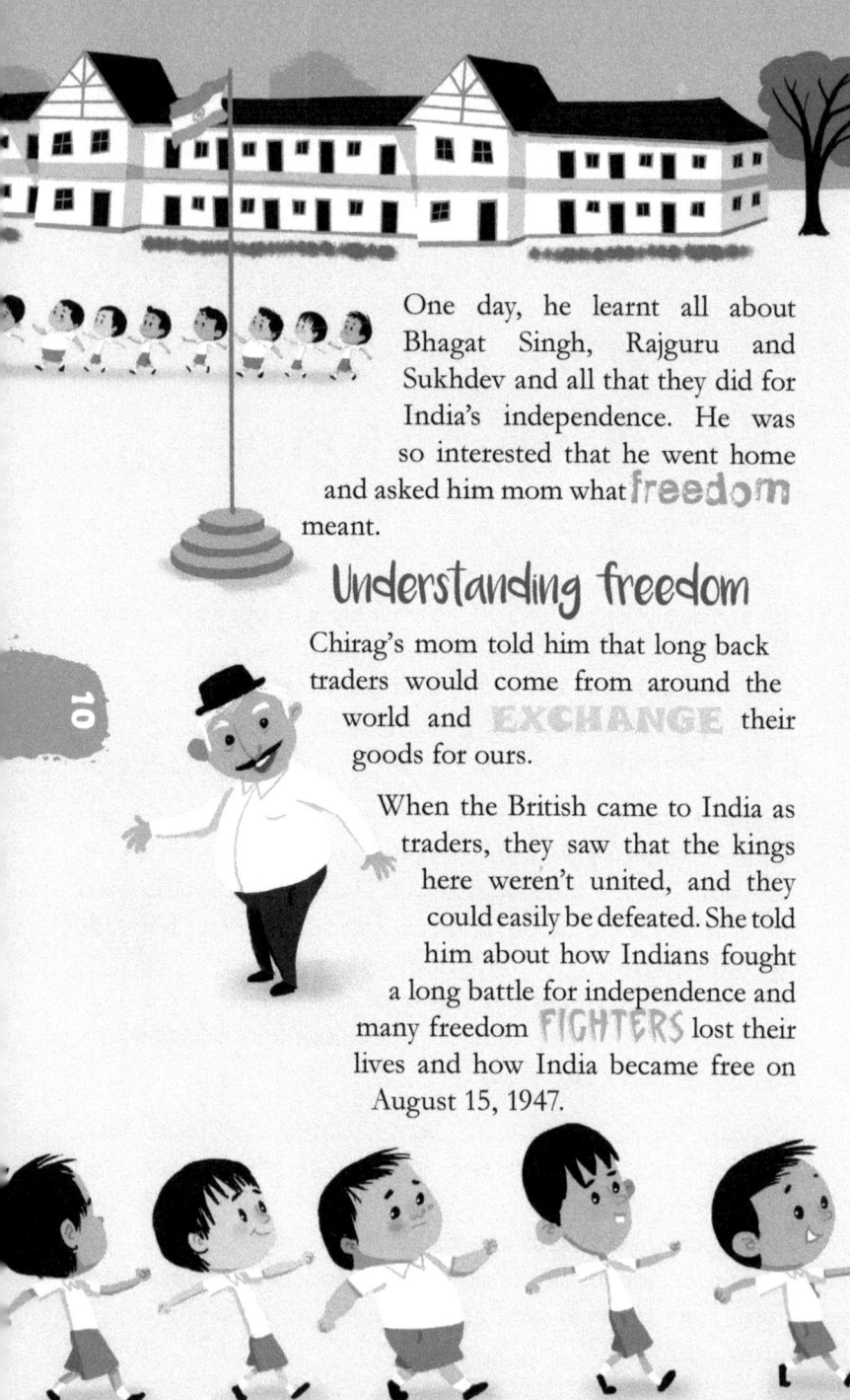

One day, he learnt all about Bhagat Singh, Rajguru and Sukhdev and all that they did for India's independence. He was so interested that he went home and asked him mom what freedom meant.

Understanding freedom

Chirag's mom told him that long back traders would come from around the world and EXCHANGE their goods for ours.

When the British came to India as traders, they saw that the kings here weren't united, and they could easily be defeated. She told him about how Indians fought a long battle for independence and many freedom FIGHTERS lost their lives and how India became free on August 15, 1947.

Chirag listened carefully and finally asked her why it was important for a country to rule itself. Chirag's mom explained that since the land we live on is ours, the GOVERNANCE of the land should also rest with us. She also explained that freedom means being able to choose your government and setting up a legal system that is equal and benefits all its citizens.

She also told him about slavery where human beings just like them didn't have the authority to do anything on their own. This made Chirag think of his pet parrot and his pet dog. He wondered whether they were free or not as his parrot was always locked in a cage and his dog was **chained** up most of the time.

Celebrating independence

Soon, the date was August 15 and it was time for the school's Independence Day celebration. Chirag put on his uniform and pinned his house badge to his chest. His hair was neat, his nails cut and his shoes were shiny. Chirag went to school.

At school, the chief guest gave a speech and hoisted the FLAG. The students stood in attention and sang the national anthem. The different houses paraded around the school grounds. They also took part in several competitions.

One of Chirag's seniors talked about freedom and why it was important. At the end of the day, it was time to give out the prizes. Chirag had won three prizes in all. One was for the best attendance, the next for being the best student and the third for the best parade which he accepted on behalf of his house.

The chief guest presented the awards to Chirag and his school principal praised him for being such a good student. Chirag was very HAPPY.

When Chirag went home, he showed the prizes to his mom. She was very happy. He also told her that he listened to his senior's SPEECH about freedom. When his dad came home from work, he showed his prizes to him as well.

The next morning, Chirag walked up to his mom and asked her if he could set his parrot free. His mom nodded and they brought the CAGE to the window. Chirag opened the door and the parrot flew up into the sky. It flew around and sat down on the branch of a tree. It looked at Chirag and his mom and CHIRPED.

Both Chirag and his mom wore big SMILES on their faces. Chirag now knew exactly what freedom was.

That's Not Right

Independence Day is celebrated on August 15. Some things in this picture are not right. Find out what they are.

Rewinding Time

By Soumitra Kanungo and Annabel George

On August 14 and 15, 1947, British India was divided into two separate countries: India and Pakistan. Muslims who were staying in India travelled to Pakistan and Hindus who were staying in Pakistan travelled to India. Many families had to take long journeys as transport was limited. Some had to walk long distances while some took several connecting buses before they could reach their destination.

A reader shares an account of her grandmother's experience during the partition of India and Pakistan

Before the Partition, my grandmother lived with her family in a district called **Rawalpindi**, presently located in Pakistan. The family of six sisters and three brothers lived in a huge house. My grandmother's family was quite well-known because her father was part of the British ARMY. She was around six or seven years old when the Partition was ANNOUNCED. Since they were Hindus, they had to leave their home in Rawalpindi and travel to New Delhi, where millions of refugees (people who are forced to leave their country) had gathered. When the time came to leave their home, my grandmother's father wasn't around. Her mother and her aunts buried some of their gold underground because they

were afraid of being robbed while travelling. They left a few other **belongings** behind in the hope that they might someday return home.

They journeyed from Rawalpindi to Delhi in a small vehicle along with other refugees. On arriving in Delhi, they received **accommodation** from the government. In fact, my grandmother's family received better facilities because her father had served in the army. They lived

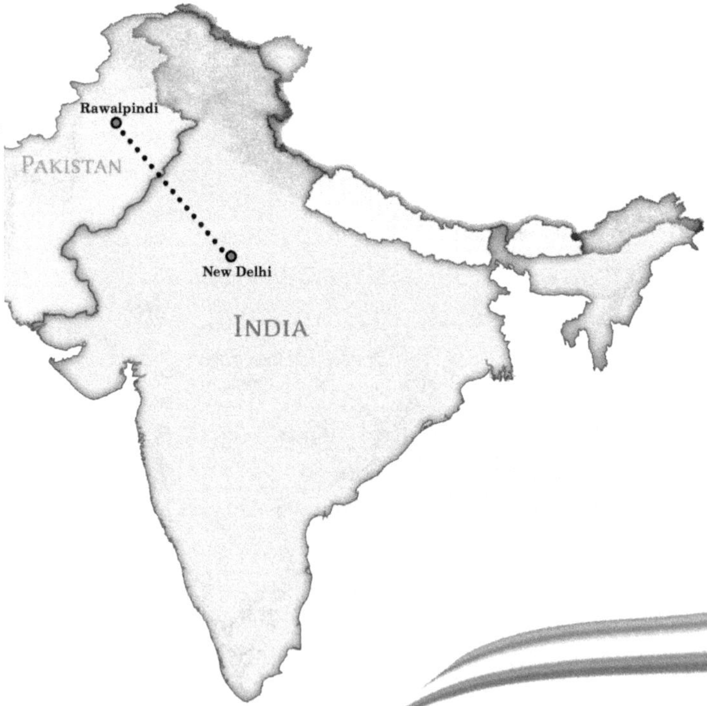

Rawalpindi

PAKISTAN

New Delhi

INDIA

like REFUGEES for about a year until the government provided them with concessions to start a business of their own.

With the Partition, my grandmother lost her home, her friends, and many other things. However, she grew closer to her sisters and mother. Each one helped the other adjust to the new ways of living. But somehow, through all of this, they lived with the never-ending HOPE of returning HOME.

Nayana Patel, a resident of Kandivali narrates a story by Gosai Bhai Patel, her father and a freedom fighter

Around the time when Mahatma Gandhi launched the Quit India Movement in 1942, my father, aged 20 years, was an ACTIVE FIGHTER. The Quit India Movement demanded complete freedom from the British rule. In his speeches, Gandhiji empowered each and every Indian to fight against the British, forcing them to QUIT India. While the TENSION in the country was rising, my father participated in several campaigns. Overcome by the sentiment to do anything for the country, he recited Quit India slogans in the neighborhood and distributed anti-British pamphlets while in hiding. He would be JAILED if he was found by the British soldiers. Even hoisting the Indian flag was PUNISHABLE.

Gosai Bhai Patel

My father took it as a challenge and also the first step towards our country's freedom. He and his companions challenged the British government by attempting to hoist India's flag on a large banyan tree. The British government set up a barrier with guards surrounding the tree to stop them. To defy the British, my father and his companions created a strategy to hoist the flag in the night. They painted their bodies black to camouflage themselves and walked silently through the nearby sugarcane fields. Two of them sneaked past the sleeping guards to reach the tree and climbed it to hoist the flag on its tallest branch. When my father and the other men in hiding saw the flag tied to the tallest branch of the tree, they shouted SLOGANS and ran away. The loud chanting woke the British soldiers from their sleep. They were SURPRISED to see the flag hoisted on the tree despite heavy barriers.

Through this attempt, they made the British realize that this was their motherland and each Indian was willing to bravely stand against the dominant British rule.

We are lucky to live in free India as now we can hoist our national flag freely in our country.

Colour Me

Importance of Voting

By Bimal Raval

Neel was very excited because he had received an invitation for the **NATIONAL VOTERS' DAY** celebration, which is celebrated on January 25 every year.

Khushi, his younger sister, asked, "Bhai, what's the matter, why are you so excited?"

"I recently turned 18, so now I can **VOTE** when elections are held. See, I got a Voter Identity card also," said Neel and showed her his card. "So, do you get more pocket money with that card?" she asked.

Neel laughed and said, "No, no. It is not a card that gives me money. I get to vote in the next elections by showing this card," he explained.

Khushi was still unable to understand why Neel was so excited about this card. It really would not matter if he did not vote!

Voting in Khushi's class

A few days later, Khushi's class teacher, Ms Anita, announced that they would have ELECTIONS for the position of the class monitor. Those who were interested would have to register their names by January 15.

Khushi wanted to become the class monitor and registered her name.

On January 15, Ms Anita announced that she had received two names for the position of the class monitor—Khushi and Dhavan.

She then showed and distributed a bunch of printed cards to the entire class.

"What are these cards, Ms Anita?" asked Dhavan.

"I have prepared a card for every student in our class. It has their **ROLL NUMBER** and name written on it. Each card is signed by me so that no one can duplicate it. We will call it a 'Voter ID card'. On the day of the election, everyone must carry their Voter IDs to school. We will be

creating a **POLLING BOOTH** in the auditorium hall and senior students will help us conduct the elections."

"Once you enter the polling booth, you will have to show your card to the person who is monitoring the polling booth. They will then give you a ballot paper for voting. This paper will contain the names of the two nominated students for the position of the class monitor."

"Then you will have to tick mark the box in front of your **PREFERRED CANDIDATE** and drop the ballot paper in the box kept at the polling booth. Anyone who is not carrying their Voter ID will not be allowed to vote." Ms Anita explained the entire voting process.

Khushi had many friends in her class and because of her helpful nature, she knew most of her classmates. Though she was a **FAVOURITE** candidate to win the elections, she held meetings with different groups of students during the lunch break and urged them to vote for her.

Dhavan too had a big group of friends, and even he started campaigning during free periods and lunch breaks, asking his classmates to vote for him.

During each meeting, he spoke about the importance of the Voter ID and reminded all his classmates to carry theirs on the voting day, because without it they would not be allowed to cast their votes.

On the day of the election, the polling booth had been set up in the auditorium hall, and senior students were helping Ms Anita to conduct the elections. But a few students, despite the daily reminders, forgot to carry their Voter IDs and weren't allowed to vote.

The announcement of the class monitor

After everyone had cast their votes, the counting of votes was done by the senior students in the presence of Ms Anita.

Khushi and Dhavan were anxiously waiting for the results. Ms Anita finally announced, "Dhavan has won the class monitor election by 2 votes. Out of 45 students, 41 students cast their votes. The remaining 4 students were not allowed to cast their votes because they forgot their Voter IDs."

Khushi was **DISAPPOINTED**. She was disheartened even more when she learnt that three of her friends had not been allowed to vote because they had forgotten to carry their Voter IDs. She was certain that those three votes could have changed the election results.

Ms Anita explained, "Some students might have thought that their vote would not make much of a difference. So they weren't serious about the Voter IDs and forgot to bring them to school. But all of you must have now realised that even a single vote can make a huge difference. That is why every year the Election Commission celebrates National Voters' Day to increase the number of voters and create awareness about our voting rights. The newly enrolled voters are handed their Voter IDs on this day."

All the students thanked Ms Anita for conducting such a **fun** and _informative_ election. And they welcomed their newly elected class monitor—Dhavan, with a huge round of applause.

Khushi realised the importance of voting and was now able to understand Neel's excitement on receiving his Voter ID.

Complete the Picture

January 25 is National Voters' Day. Parts of this image have been left blank. Look at the picture, complete it and then colour it.

Children's Council

By Bimal Raval

Loknath, the headman of Gokul Village, was addressing the Gram Sabha, clarifying and answering queries raised by the villagers.

At the end of the meeting, Loknath proposed the children of the village be able to have their voices heard along with the adults. All the villagers were surprised, and asked how.

"There is a way that children can raise the concerns related to them through a democratic platform called the **BAL PANCHAYAT**—Children's Council," Loknath explained. "The children elect representatives who are between 10 and 18 years old, and those representatives will form the Council. They will meet periodically to discuss issues relevant to them, and give the Gram Panchayat a list of their most important concerns for further action."

Most of the villagers thought it was a strange idea, but surprisingly many children said that they were interested in forming a Bal Panchayat.

Loknath was happy to see that children wanted to participate. "Good!" he said.

The formation of the Bal Panchayat

"While I compile a list of eligible voters, you register your nominations with the Panchayat Office. Remember, you'll need an equal number of boy and girl candidates. Every candidate will complete a declaration form and use a copy of it for campaigning, which can be done through meetings or going door-to-door. One day before the election, a ballot will be sent to every eligible voter. The expenses of the election will be borne by the Bal Panchayat Commission."

After the Bal Panchayat Commission received the nominations, the members announced the election date and gave the candidates two days to campaign. The election was held at the Panchayat Office. All the eligible voters cast their vote by putting a **stamp** against the name of their candidate.

After counting all the votes, the results were announced. Khushi was elected to the top position of Sarpanch, and Param became the Deputy Sarpanch of the Bal Panchayat. Neel, Shivani, and Gopal were elected as core committee members. All elected members received a certificate and identity card valid for one year. Loknath explained their roles and responsibilities.

Soon came the first **INDEPENDENT** Bal Panchayat meeting.

Khushi opened the meeting. "Friends, we are here to identify the issues we need to work on."

"Some people are not concerned about their health," Neel noted. "We need to create **awareness** about the use of toilets and regular **polio** drops for kids, and the problem of **MALNUTRITION** among young kids and mothers."

Gopal added, "We need to create awareness about the wastage of water."

"So, how do we create awareness?" Khushi asked.

Shivani said, "We can explain the importance of health by organizing a few plays, with each play focusing on one subject, like the health benefits of using toilets, or the separation of wet and dry waste. There could be a play on the effects of polio to create awareness about polio drops."

Neel jumped up. "I will play the lead role!" he said excitedly.

"Okay, but calm down," Khushi said. "Everybody will have to participate because we need to organize at least four to five different plays on different occasions."

Param said, "I think if we try to explain to people, especially elders, they won't listen to us. We need to make it interesting, so to convince them, we need to do some homework on these topics."

With eyebrows raised, Gopal asked, "HOMEWORK? We need to do homework here, like at school?"

Param smiled. "No, Gopal, not that kind of homework! But yes, with the help of the internet, we'll need to get rough data about water wastage and other topics. On June 5, which is Environment Day, we can organize a tree-planting program where we can share this data."

Khushi was impressed with Param's idea for convincing the elders with facts and figures. She said, "That's great! I have an idea for conducting a few awareness sessions on MALNUTRITION for women with the help of Doctor Priyesh, who works at the Public Health Center."

"As for education, you all might have observed that many students drop out," Shivani remarked. "We should also campaign for increasing school enrollment this year."

The council runs in full swing

After some more discussion, the members of the Bal Panchayat agreed on the action plan.

Over the next few months, the COUNCIL was active in putting on plays on the topics they'd come up with in the first meeting. Malnutrition sessions conducted with the help of Dr. Priyesh initially got a low response, but later, they made it more interactive and included some fun games. That made it popular, and they received an overwhelming response.

On Environment Day, they organized a mass tree-planting program. Khushi and Param presented the data about the

water **WASTAGE**. The villagers were shocked by the figures, and all **pLedged** to save water for future.

The Bal Panchayat, with Loknath's help, launched an education **AWARENESS** campaign to address the school dropout issue and increase new school enrollments. They contacted some of the parents to remind them to regularly send their children to school.

In a few months, the villagers saw visible changes from the Bal Panchayat's activities. The village was **ALIVE** with various **ACTIVITIES**, and Gokul Village was nominated for an award.

All the villagers appreciated the Bal Panchayat's efforts and thanked Loknath for introducing the Bal Panchayat in their village.

Complete the Picture

Parts of this image have been left blank. Look at the picture, complete it and then colour it.

A Nation's Identity

By Renuka Shrivastav

On the eve of Republic Day, Aamir went to the MARKET with his father to buy paper flags to put up in his house. Whenever he bought anything for himself, he would also buy one for his younger brother Wasim.

As soon as he reached home, Aamir stuck a flag by the gate, and gave the other to his brother. "Stick your flag too, Wasim. That way, both our flags will be FLUTTERING in the air and it will look nice," said Aamir.

"No, I will not stick my flag here. I will stick it on the hood of our car. That way whenever Baba drives the car, the flag will flutter," said Wasim.

"No, Wasim. You can't do that," said Aamir.

Wasim does not listen

"You bought it for me and I will do whatever I want with it," said Wasim and ran towards the car.

Aamir ran behind him but Wasim tripped and fell down. He immediately started crying. When Aamir tried to help him, Wasim pushed his hand away.

"Go away! I will not talk to you. You **PUSHED** me on purpose," said Wasim wailing.

Hearing Wasim crying, their mother rushed towards him and asked, "What happened? Why are you crying?"

"Aamir pushed me, Ma!" said Wasim.

"No, I did not! He is lying. He wanted to stick the flag on the car but I told him not to. He didn't listen to me and ran towards the car and fell down," said Aamir.

"Wasim, why don't you listen to your brother?" asked Ma.

"Why should I listen to him? He bought this flag for me and I can do whatever I want with it," said Wasim.

"Son, it is our national flag and is a **symbol** of our country. There are certain rules to using the flag. Your brother knows about it and he tried to tell you about it," said Ma.

"What is wrong in sticking the flag to the hood of the car?" asked Wasim.

"There is something called the Flag Code of India which states the rules and practices with regards to the display of the national flag. And one of the rules states that only **IMPORTANT HEADS** of the government like president, vice-president, prime

minister, governors and the chief justice of India can fly the flag on their vehicles," said Ma.

"Why is that so?" asked Wasim curiously.

"Laying down the rules on the usage of the national flag helps preserve its respect and dignity," said Ma.

"Why is it important to preserve the dignity of the flag?" asked Wasim.

"Son, each country has its own identity represented by the national flag. Our country's identity is our national flag. Respecting the flag means respecting our country and the people who fought for its identity. Our country gained FREEDOM from the British after a lot of struggle. The cost of freedom was the lives of several freedom fighters and the sacrifices they made. Because of them, we finally gained independence from the British on August 15, 1947," explained Ma.

"Then what is Republic Day celebrated for?" asked Wasim.

"January 26 is the date when the Constitution was formally adopted by the Indian parliament," answered Aamir.

The Constitution

"What is the constitution?" asked Wasim.

"Let me simplify this for you. We had got our freedom from the British but we were still following their rules and laws. Our own set of laws needed to be written. So, a committee headed by Dr. B. R. Ambedkar drafted our country's own rules and legislations that we began to follow from January 26, 1950. That is when our country became a republic wherein the power is with the people and their elected representatives," explained Ma. "That is why that day is celebrated with great pomp and show in New Delhi in front of the president of India."

"Our school has also planned special programmes tomorrow!" said Wasim excitedly.

"So, now do you understand why you should not play with the national flag?" asked Ma.

"Yes, Ma. Thanks for explaining everything to me clearly. If I had known all this information earlier I wouldn't have played with the flag," said Wasim.

"That is what your brother tried to tell you. Next time, just listen to what he has to say before you go running away," said Ma smiling.

"I will, Ma," said Wasim. He then turned to Aamir and asked, "Will you help me stick this flag on our GATE?"

"OF COURSE, I will, little brother. And let's plan our own Republic Day celebration at home," said Aamir.

"Yes, let's! This will be our own way of showing respect to our country," said Wasim beaming.

Tricolour Badge

By Pooja Nandanwar

You will need:

Orange, white and green chart papers, pencil, scissors, glue, blue sketch pen, safety pin

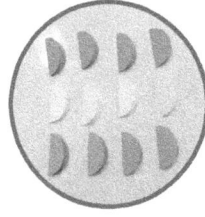

1. Cut 4 circles each using orange, white and green chart papers. Fold them in half.

2. Layer the folded orange, white and green circles, as shown in the image, and glue them together.

3. Cut strips of the same colours and glue them at the back of the badge.

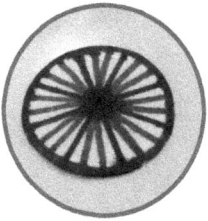

4. Roll and glue a piece of paper in the center to give support to the Ashoka chakra.

5. Design the chakra using blue sketch pen and glue it.

The tricolour badge is ready!

6. Using a piece of paper, glue a safety pin at the back.

A True Patriot

By Kumud Kumar

Aunt Sheena and Mini were neighbours. One morning when Aunt Sheena saw Mini carrying an Indian flag to Azad Park, she was curious and inquired, "WHY ARE YOU CARRYING THE FLAG, MINI?"

"Aunt Sheena, our flag is a symbol of our patriotism and I am carrying it to show that I am patriotic," replied Mini.

"Oh, that is WONDERFUL!" Aunt Sheena said, encouraging her.

"Can you please suggest what else I can do to become a patriot? Our freedom fighters Subhash Chandra Bose, Bhagat Singh, and Chandrashekhar Azad fought the British and became known as patriots. I don't know whom I should fight to be called a patriot," said Mini.

Aunt Sheena smiled at Mini's *innocence*. "Mini, you don't have to fight anyone to be patriotic. You can show your love for your country in other ways."

"What can I do so my name can go on the list of our country's patriots?" asked Mini.

"Well, you could help the POOR OR ASSIST THE

ELDERLY," began Aunt Sheena. "Or you could help save the environment by planting more TREES, or teach poor children for free. This way, you can serve your country and be called a patriot."

Aunt Sheena's words had a huge impact on Mini. She instantly thought of the poor family that lived close to her house. Mini always saw the daughter, Parul, engaged in household work and never saw her play in the park. She always wondered who helped Parul with her studies.

Mini decided she would tutor Parul, and a few days later she went to her house.

"Hello, aunty," Mini greeted Parul's mother. "I live in the neighbouring society, and my name is Mini. Is it okay if I come in? I wanted to speak to you."

Once Mini was inside, she said, "Aunty, I noticed Parul is always busy with housework. Does she get enough time to study? I am willing to help her if she needs it."

"You are so kind, Mini. But Parul doesn't like studying. She helps me with the **HOUSEHOLD CHORES** and sometimes helps her father at the shop," Parul's mother responded.

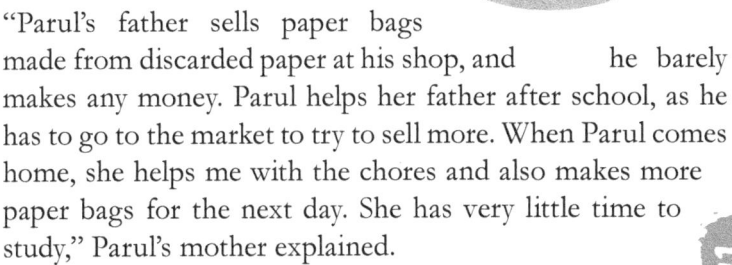

"But, aunty, she is my age. Shouldn't she be studying?" asked Mini.

"Parul's father sells paper bags made from discarded paper at his shop, and he barely makes any money. Parul helps her father after school, as he has to go to the market to try to sell more. When Parul comes home, she helps me with the chores and also makes more paper bags for the next day. She has very little time to study," Parul's mother explained.

"I understand, aunty. But this could be the reason she doesn't like studying. If you don't mind, can I teach her on holidays?" asked Mini.

Parul's mother smiled. "I appreciate your concern for Parul. I'll ask her if she would like you to tutor her on holidays," she said.

Mini becomes a teacher

Soon after Mini began her tutoring sessions, Parul started enjoying learning new things, and she understood the subjects better.

A little help from Mini had cultivated Parul's interest in studies, and soon she started studying on her own whenever she had time. She even studied during her spare time in her father's shop. Gradually, her confidence grew and she began answering questions in class. Her grades improved, which drew the attention of her principal, Ms. Saloni.

"Parul, you have been working very hard. **HOW DID YOU MANAGE ALL THIS**?" asked Ms. Saloni.

"Ma'am, my friend Mini, has been helping me for some time now. She teaches me for free. After they saw how I improved, many other families have asked Mini to teach their kids" replied Parul.

Ms. Saloni was quite happy to hear this. That year, Parul topped her class. She also won a scholarship and ₹5,000 for her performance in her final exams. Parul's parents were happy, and started paying more attention to her education.

On the morning of Independence Day, Ms. Saloni visited Mini's house and after getting permission from her parents, she took Mini to Ms. Saloni's own school.

The school was *decorated* beautifully for the occasion. "Ma'am, isn't this the same government school that Parul and her friends attend?" asked Mini.

"Yes, Mini, and we will all celebrate Independence Day here today," replied Ms. Saloni.

As they entered the school, the head girl, who was also hosting the program, said to the gathered students, "Friends, let us all extend a warm welcome to our guests, and a very special welcome to our chief guest, Mini. She will be HOISTING the flag here today."

Mini was taken aback. Ms. Saloni said, "Yes, Mini. You will be hoisting the flag today."

Mini could not understand why she was being given so much respect.

As she hoisted the flag, the whole school chanted, "Jai Hind!" This was followed by the national anthem and a few cultural programs. Mini was seated alongside Ms. Saloni.

A dream come true

At the end of the program, Ms. Saloni was invited on the stage to give a speech.

"Children, today we celebrate our Independence Day, honouring our great freedom fighters, but I am pleased to tell you that there are still some patriots among us who are serving our country without any expectation of a reward. We have one such patriot among us today. Mini has been serving our country selflessly in her own special way. It is our duty to honour such patriots and give them the respect that they truly deserve," she said.

Then Ms. Saloni explained how Mini had been teaching poor children in her spare time. She mentioned that Mini was fighting a war against poverty and brightening up the lives of children like Parul.

Mini was EMOTIONAL.

The entire school applauded Mini for her service to her country. This brought tears to Mini's eyes—her dream of becoming a patriot had finally come true.

Memory

January 26 is Republic Day. Look at the picture and answer the following questions.

Q1. How many flags can you count?

Q2. What float have the Champakvan animals made?

Q3. What else is happening at the Republic Day parade?

From Mohandas to Mahatma

TRACING HIS JOURNEY

Letter to Bapu

Dear Bapu,

Please accept my humble greetings.

I was born on December 26, 1947. Thirty-five days later, that is, on **January 30, 1948**, you passed away. I did not have the good fortune to meet you.

In school, I read a lot about you in my textbooks. I took part in elocution competitions on your birthday. In these **competitions**, I won prizes as well as honour.

When I grew a little older, I read your book about your life, *My Experiments With Truth*. I was so touched by it that I decided to share this book with other people.

Till date, I have shared more than 1,000 copies of the book with school **libraries** and with children on their birthdays. I shall continue doing so till the very end.

I have been **inspired** by your book and I am doing my bit to inspire many other children of our nation to be like you. I hope that it will bring **PEACE** to you, wherever you are.

I learnt from you how we can **APOLOGISE** for our **MISDEEDS**. The truth can be **CHALLENGED**, but cannot be wished away—that is what you taught me.

Today I continue to accept my mistakes and seek **forgiveness**. You have taught me the importance

46

of **TIDINESS**, so I always keep my cupboard clean. You taught me the importance of preserving the environment, I am careful in my use of paper.

I reply to all the letters I get. I go for morning walks regularly. I only buy clothes when necessary.

When I had to teach my friends the importance of **PUNCTUALITY**, I looked to you for lessons. I learnt that you had given up sugar for fifteen days before advising a little girl to do the same. I too reach my classes before time for fifteen days, and then advised others to be punctual. I could explain the advantages of punctuality through my personal experience.

Inspired by your **social service**, I have written books on various subjects for the betterment of students. I hope that I've improved the careers of some children through my books.

I donated blood 58 times to help the sick and the diseased.

There is so much strength in one's promise to oneself. I believe that my homage to you through this letter will definitely help people like me.

I want to learn to live by your **values**.

Yours sincerely,

A student of India

Colour Me

48

A Narrow Escape

By Kumud Kumar

Mahatma Gandhi's revolutionary and Satyagrahi life actually began in the country of South Africa.

A terrifying incident happened in Durban, South Africa.

Gandhi reached the port of Durban with his wife and children aboard the steamer SS Courtland along with a lot of other Indians on **December 18, 1896**. Yet, for various reasons, including a medical checkup, they were only allowed to disembark on January 13, 1897.

The white people in Durban were angry with Gandhi for two reasons.

On one hand, they believed that in India, Gandhi had unnecessarily criticised the residents of Natal, South Africa. On the other, they suspected Gandhi wanted to fill Natal with an Indian population and had brought two ships full of Indians as a result.

Both these allegations were false. However, the Courtland steamer's captain was informed that Gandhi could only leave the ship after sunset for his own safety.

On the same day, Durban's famous judge, Mr Latton, reached Gandhi's 𝕊𝕋𝔼𝔸𝕄𝔼ℝ. He advised Gandhi that he should let his family go to Jeevanji Rustom's house, an Indian businessman belonging to the Parsi community, by a car and that Latton and Gandhi would walk there. Gandhi agreed.

Gandhi and a violent mob

At 4:30PM, after sending his family off in the car, Gandhi got off the ship and started walking with Judge Latton.

Rustom's house was 3 km away and it would take one hour on foot.

But as soon as Gandhi came out of the port, people recognised him by his distinctive hat.

They started shouting, "**GANDHI! GANDHI! BEAT HIM! BEAT HIM! CATCH HIM!**" Hearing the noise, a crowd gathered. Some of them began throwing stones, pebbles and rotten eggs at him.

Judge Latton realised that walking would be risky, and he quickly called for a rickshaw.

But the people scared the rickshaw puller by threatening him, "If you let him ride in your rickshaw, we will beat you and will BREAK your rickshaw."

The scared rickshaw puller, muttered, "khaa (No)," and fled.

For Latton and Gandhi, there was no other way than to walk. The mob of whites increased, and a tall, bulky man separated Latton from Gandhi.

The rain of stones and pebbles being thrown at Gandhi increased. Amidst the scuffle, somebody pulled off Gandhi's hat and threw him to the ground.

What happened next was even scarier. Another big, bulky white man came towards Gandhi, slapped his face sharply, kicked him and shoved him to the ground.

Gandhi was about to fall, but his hands found a fence of a house, and he held ground.

Taking a breath, he moved ahead. He had no hope of ESCAPING the rough mob, who were continuously slapping him.

Alexander to the rescue

Meanwhile, a police officer's wife, Mrs Alexander, was passing by. She knew Gandhi. She came to him and opened her UMBRELLA and covered him. She then started walking alongside him.

THE MOB WOULD NOT ATTACK A WHITE WOMAN and a police officer's wife, yet they continued hurting Gandhi without hitting her.

On seeing this, an Indian youth informed Chief Constable Richard Alexander at the police station that Gandhi was being attacked while walking with Mr Alexander's wife. Mr Alexander immediately sent a force to save Gandhi and brought him to the station.

He advised Gandhi to stay at the station and left for Rustom's house without any difficulty.

A doctor examined Gandhi's wounds and began treating him. One wound was quite painful and bleeding. The doctor advised Gandhi to rest, but the commotion outside Rustom's house would not allow that.

Hundreds of white people had gathered outside Rustom's house. Some hooligans threatened Rustom by saying, "If you don't give us Gandhi, we will set fire to your house and shops."

Chief Constable Alexander became aware of this new situation. He arrived secretly with his officers. He ordered a bench and started talking to the mob while standing on it.

He covered the doors of Rustom's house so that no one could go in.

Alexander placed secret service

men at different spots in the crowd and also ordered an officer to wear Indian clothes and darken his face, so he looked like an Indian.

After that, he sent a message to Gandhi saying that if he wanted his friend Rustom's house and family to be safe, Gandhi should do as he said and dress in the clothes of an Indian constable.

Gandhi agreed and put on a **constable's uniform**. To protect his head from injury, he put a bronze saucer on it and covered it with a headcloth.

He then went along with the officer who was dressed as an Indian businessman. Another policeman accompanied them.

They took some bags of cement from a nearby shop and made their way through the crowd. A car sent by Alexander was waiting for them on the corner. Gandhi got in and reached the police station safely while the mob was unaware of his escape.

While Gandhi was making his way through the mob, Alexander had kept them busy chanting slogans: "Let's hang Gandhi! Let's hang Gandhi!"

When Alexander received the news of Gandhi's safe arrival at the police station, he addressed the crowd, "Your target has already escaped from this house!"

The mob was stunned. Some were angry, some laughing, and some could not believe how it could have happened.

Alexander told them, "If you can find Gandhi in Rustom's house, I will give him to you. You can choose to do whatever you want with him."

A group of three or four from the mob searched every corner of the house, but could not find Gandhi.

The news of Gandhi being lynched reached the British government and Colonial Secretary Joseph Chamberlain ordered action against the rioters. However, Gandhi requested against the action.

"The attackers were young, they got confused with wrong news," he wrote to the government. Gandhi always quoted Jesus in saying hate the sin and not the sinner.

Map Quest

The birth of Mahatma Gandhi is celebrated on October 2 as Gandhi Jayanti. Students of a school are unhappy and have decided to stand for their rights. Help Zoya to choose the correct group which highlights Gandhian values and principles to put their rights.

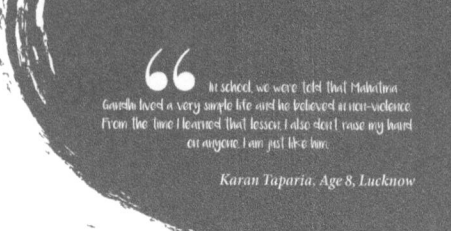

Growing Up a Gandhi

By Tushar Gandhi

Ever since I can remember, I have always received a double greeting. Introduced as "Meet Tushar Gandhi…" I would usually be met with a very casual "Hello." Then my companion would say, "…the great-grandson of Mahatma Gandhi," and my hand would be grasped respectfully. Such a reaction is SATISFYING as well as humbling—I am proud that I get this respect, but it also brings home the fact that it comes to me not because I earned it, but because I was born into the family of Mahatma Gandhi, the father of our nation.

I was born long after Mohandas Karamchand Gandhi, or "Bapu" (as he is affectionately called in India), was assassinated; I did not have any direct contact with him. My grandfather, Manilal Gandhi, the second son of Bapu and his wife, Kasturba, had also passed away before my birth.

I grew up on a diet of bedtime stories about the interactions that my father, Arun, my grandmother, Sushila, and Aunt

Ela had with "Mota Ba" (Kasturba) and Bapu. As a child, sometimes I would get fed up of these stories and would demand that I be told regular fairy tales, like all other children. Today I am thankful for these family stories, because I remember them and understand them better. These stories have molded my present-day beliefs, and have helped me lead a more **FRUITFUL** life.

A blunder that could not be forgiven

Once, in school, I was asked when India gained her independence. I blurted out that we became independent on August 15, 1948, when the correct date is August 15, 1947. Immediately after giving the WRONG answer, I realized my error and tried to make amends, but my teacher and my classmates were shocked. In their eyes, I had made a grave mistake: how could Gandhiji's great-grandson not know the answer to this simple question? I apologized profusely, I confessed that it was a slip of the tongue, but there was no forgiveness. The matter was reported to our principal and I was promptly sent home from school. I had to take my father to school to meet the principal, who was a freedom fighter and a very devout follower of Bapu. When he told my father about my mistake, there were tears in his eyes. I was not to be forgiven.

I was spoken to severely, and had to stay after school each day for a month. During DETENTION, my principal gave me lessons in history. After this I was allowed to go back to normal activities, but the hurt in my principal's eyes and the ANGER in my history teacher remained for a long time. Good grades and good behaviour could not wash away the blunder I had committed.

Ups and downs

Being the great grandson of Bapu had advantages, too. I escaped punishment at school for mischief I committed. While growing up, I realized that many things happened to me just because I was Bapu's great-grandson. I am sure he would not have approved.

At the same time, everything I did was watched. One day, at a public function, I had CHICKEN on my plate. Seeing this, a complete stranger told me that I was betraying Bapu, who was a strict vegetarian. Even when I was fighting the Lok Sabha elections in 1998, my party had told two of my friends to keep me away from the non-vegetarian food at the Iftar parties, where JOURNALISTS were always present.

Dandi March and my family

All my life I have been fascinated by the fact that three generations of my family had joined the historic Dandi March of 1930. Although it took us 17 more years to gain independence, it was after the Salt March and subsequent Salt Satyagraha that the British lost their moral superiority over us.

My grandfather Manilal was among the 80 people Bapu had picked from the Ashram residents to walk with him. Another man in the march was Harilal Gandhi's son, my father's cousin Kantilal. They had walked in defiance of the British monopoly over the manufacture and sale of salt and the UNFAIR 1,400% tax they had imposed on it. My family walked from Sabarmati Ashram, Ahmedabad, to the beachhead at Dandi.

The trek from Ahmedabad to Dandi is 241 miles long; I would often wonder if I had it in me to walk it. It was daunting, more so for a person like me, who was not known to be PHYSICALLY ACTIVE.

Finally, in 2005, on the 75th anniversary of the original march, I gathered my courage and followed in the footsteps of my ancestors. I walked from Sabarmati Ashram, Ahmedabad, to Dandi. I, too, walked, and remembered that day.

On the very next day, I had blisters on my feet. By the end of the week, the soles of my feet were two big blisters. I had blisters in between my toes, too. There were times when I was absolutely exhausted and felt like quitting. My feet would cry out for mercy—not another step! Then my heart would speak, or maybe my SOUL, or the same inner voice that spoke to Bapu. "Just one more step," and then, "One more."

Taking those single steps, I finally reached **DANDI**. Here, on the 6th of April, 1930, Bapu had picked up a fistful of saline mud and declared that the British **monopoly** on salt was broken. Bapu's **companions** had then distilled the fistful of saline mud and got roughly 10 grams of salt from it. It was this experience that taught me that the strength of one's promise is much stronger than one's muscles.

The legacy of being a Gandhi

Looking back as a child, my grandmother, Ba, explained my legacy to me thus: "Tushar, you are like a **SAPLING** that has sprouted at the base of a great tree which casts a huge shadow. No matter what you do, you will never be able to move out of the shadow. For some this can be a **CURSE**. They will resent it and it will affect their **growth**. They could be stunted and **shrivelled**. But you could also treat it as a **boon**, a shelter. In its refuge you can thrive. Now it's up to you how you want to treat it, as a curse or as a blessing." I have always considered my lineage to be a blessing. Under the shadow of the Mahatma, I have **BLOSSOMED**.

Growing up a Gandhi may not have been easy, but it has definitely been a privilege.

Sequence

The Civil Disobedience Movement which started in 1930, was India's first large-scale, non-violent protest against the British Rule. Can you put the sequence of events in order?

1. Indian National Congress declares its objective to attain self-rule for India.

2. The Dandi March helped unite the citizens of India and was a major step towards achieving independence.

3. Following Gandhiji's march at Dandi, civil disobedience movements started all across India.

4. As a step towards self-rule, Gandhiji writes to Lord Irwin, the Viceroy, about his decision to oppose the salt tax with a march.

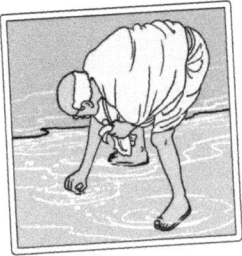

5. Gandhiji goes to the seashore at Dandi and collects salt as a sign of protest against the salt tax.

6. Gandhiji and his followers begin marching from Sabarmati Ashram to Dandi on March 12, 1930.

Fannu and Mannu

By Sonali Garge

Fannu and Mannu were twin brothers who lived in a joint family in their village. They were extremely fond of their cousin, Jugnu, who was five years older than them and they played together every day after school.

Diwali VACATION was around the corner. Everyone was waiting for Aunt Champa from Mumbai who was coming with her children, Aakash and Suhani to spend Diwali with the family.

An exciting day

On the last day of school, the three boys rushed home to meet Aunt Champa and their cousins who were coming that day. "Who wants to go to the station to receive Aunt Champa?" asked Uncle Pramod.

"Me, me...," chorused the children.

"Okay, okay! Let's all go," laughed Uncle Pramod. They all reached the station on time and waited for the train to come to the platform.

Mannu was getting **RESTLESS**. He kept looking left and right, not sure which side the train would come from. "Where is the train?" he asked the umpteenth time. Just then, they heard a loud honk of the train. Fannu and Mannu jumped with joy!

Fannu jumped so high that one of his slippers FELL on the tracks.

"How did your slipper fall, Fannu? Now you won't be able to get it back and papa will be angry. This is the third pair you have lost in two weeks," warned Mannu.

"I don't know how the slipper fell. I just jumped," said a scared Fannu. Jugnu too saw Fannu's slipper fall and laughed.

"Why are you laughing, bhaiya? Please tell me what to do. Ma and papa will be very angry with me," cried Fannu.

Mahatma Gandhi's funny tale

"Well, once Mahatma Gandhi was travelling by train. While he was boarding, one of his slippers fell on the tracks just like that. Do you know what he did then?"

"What did he do?" asked the twins together. "HE THREW AWAY HIS OTHER SLIPPER TOO!" said Jugnu.

"You too throw away your other slipper!" said Jugnoo MOCKINGLY.

The twins did not know what to say. They couldn't understand why Jugnu was asking them to throw the other slipper. Aunt Champa who reached the platform, heard and said, "Jugnu is right! Gandhi did that so that the person who found one slipper would get a pair rather than being left with one." Reluctantly Fannu picked up his ANOTHER slipper and threw it next to the one that had fallen on the track.

As soon as they left the station, Aunt Champa BOUGHT Fannu a new pair of slippers with a BUCKLE so that they wouldn't come off his feet.

The twins left, deeper in thought as they had learnt something new about Gandhi

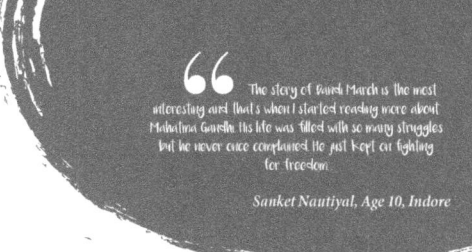

Different Roles of Gandhi

We see Mahatma Gandhi as the leader of the Indian freedom movement—his reputation as a **NON-VIOLENT** leader is imprinted in our minds and has shaped our perspective of him. He was primarily a lawyer, but whenever there was a need, he took up a new role. There are several untold stories that give us a peek into the different roles Gandhi played in his life. Here are a few.

Gandhi as a cook

At age 18, Gandhi tried his hand in the kitchen for the first time when he lived in England. He was a vegetarian, which was a new concept to the people of England—at meals he was served mostly bread, butter, and boiled vegetables. He found this food to be tasteless, and badly missed the delicious cuisine prepared by his mother, Putlibai. For some months, he managed by eating the bland English food. Then he rented his own place and had a stove installed to cook for himself.

When he returned to Mumbai after becoming a lawyer, he stayed in a small apartment. He hired a cook, but Gandhi often cooked his meals with him. Gandhi also taught his cook to prepare some English vegetarian dishes.

Mahadev Bhai, his personal secretary, once asked him, "Bapuji, did you have a cook before you went to the Phoenix Settlement?"

Gandhi replied, "No, I had left him long before. He was a good cook, but could not cook food without spices. So, I dismissed him and did not keep any cook."

Gandhi liked to experiment with different types of diets. Because of this, he ate only fruits for five years, and there was also a time he ate only SPROUTED grains and uncooked food. He tried to get others to join him, as he believed food should not be eaten for taste, but to keep the body healthy.

In his autobiography, *The Story of My Experiments with Truth*, Gandhi wrote that one of his followers said, "Recent research states that grass has a lot of VITAMINS. Fortunately, this was not known when Gandhi was in the Ashram. Otherwise, he would have shut down the Ashram kitchen and we would have been asked to graze on grass in the field."

Gandhi as an English teacher

Gandhi met many Indians in South Africa. When he organized a meeting with them, he learned that many did not know **English**. Recognizing the knowledge of English would be beneficial, Gandhi advised them that they should try to learn whenever they had **FREE** time. He took up the **RESPONSIBILITY** of teaching them.

Among them were a barber, a workman, and a Hindu shopkeeper. Because they were busy with work, Gandhi agreed to teach them in their homes. All his students **MANAGED** to learn English. Some became **PROFICIENT** and were able to correspond in English, and some were able to get better jobs because they knew the language.

Gandhi as a toilet cleaner

During the plague epidemic in Mumbai, Gandhi made sure to teach people about the importance of keeping their toilets clean, and he traveled around the city inspecting toilets. In South Africa, he emphasized **toilet CLEANLINESS** wherever he stayed. (He had done the same at the Phoenix Settlement.) Gandhi happily volunteered to clean toilets, which was considered a dirty job. Gradually, other people also came forward and helped him. At **SEVAGRAM ASHRAM** in Maharashtra, even small children brought buckets to help him clean toilets.

When Gandhi was practicing law in **DURBAN**, South Africa, his clerks lived with him. Because Gandhi's house had no drains, special vessels were kept in the rooms for passing and collecting urine. Some clerks who considered the house their own did not mind picking up their vessel to empty it; however, one clerk found it disrespectful and thought it was the duty of domestic servants. Gandhi and his wife, Kasturba, did it themselves.

Gandhi as a nurse

One day, a person suffering from **LEPROSY** came begging at Gandhi's house. Gandhi could simply have given him food and sent him away, but his conscience did not allow him to do that. Gandhi kept the leper in his room, **WASHED** his wounds, and nursed him. Gandhi could not keep him in his house for very long because he neither had the necessary FACILITIES nor the courage for the task, so he sent the man to a hospital for poor bonded laborers. This did not satisfy him, though—he had a strong desire to serve others. He started working in a hospital run on donations from Parsee Rustomji, a businessman and PHILANTHROPIST, as a nurse.

Also, during the days of the Boer War, Gandhi assisted with bringing wounded soldiers back from the battlefield and dressing their wounds.

Gandhi as a barber

Once, a thought came to Gandhi: men manage to shave, but can a man learn to give himself a haircut? With this question in mind, he went to a BARBERSHOP in Pretoria, South Africa. The barber not only refused to give him a haircut,

but also insulted him. This hurt Gandhi very much. He bought a hair-cutting machine from the market and cut his own hair, standing in front of a mirror. Gandhi managed to cut the hair in the front, but cutting the hair at the back of his head proved difficult. He could not trim it straight. When he arrived at the court, people started laughing at him. They asked him if mice had chewed off his hair. Gandhi replied, "No: how could a white barber touch my black hair? Therefore, however I look, I like my haircut as I did it with my OWN hands."

Map Quest

To celebrate Gandhi Jayanti on October 2, Mayank has to dress like Gandhi for a fancy-dress competition in school. Help him pick the right costume.

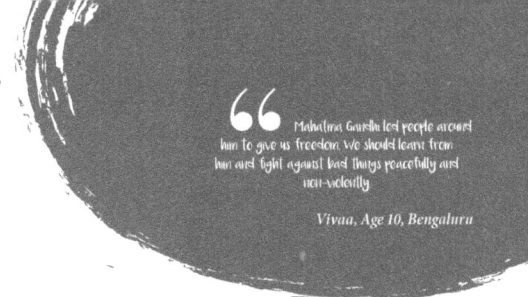
Hard Work Pays Off

By Dr K Rani

Nine-year-old Aisha lived with her parents in a small Uttarakhand hilltop district called Sudoor. Aisha's father worked as a primary school teacher in the village.

The villagers called him **Masterji** out of love and respect. The school was attended by students not only from his village, but from many surrounding ones as well.

Aisha's village was located a small distance from the main road. Once, the state government was connecting this road to the rest of the village.

Under the authority of a local dealer, **labourers** from another state had been employed to cut through the hill and construct a connecting road to the village.

It was the first time the labourers had been employed in the area. They weren't well acquainted with the local language.

The dealer had much difficulty giving instructions to the labourers and often expressed his frustration over them.

When the labourers visited a shop to buy construction materials, the shopkeeper would not sell them anything because of the language gap too.

Masterji often observed the labourers while passing through the road. From his appearance and overall personality, they knew that he was a schoolteacher. And so, each time he passed, they greeted him respectfully.

One day, Masterji was purchasing some things from a shop. Just then, one of the labourers entered the shop and asked for some material from the shopkeeper.

Masterji's new students

But as usual, the shopkeeper didn't understand a word and denied the request. Masterji felt quite sad and disappointed. He decided to teach the basics of their **LOCAL LANGUAGE** to the labourers.

He thought that this would offer them some ease and comfort in this strange place. He communicated his idea to them. Since they didn't have any free time during the day, he could only teach them at the construction site in the evening. Sometimes, he had to wait for hours for them to finish their day's work.

Aisha didn't like this at all. In the evening, she usually went for a walk in the park with her father. He used to narrate interesting stories to her. But nowadays, her father's attention was totally directed towards teaching the labourers.

On the other hand, Masterji's efforts were beginning to **reap results**. The labourers were beginning to understand and speak the local language.

Seeing him happy, one day Aisha asked, "Papa, you seem happier today."

"Yes. The labourers are beginning to learn our local language."

"But Papa, because of the labourers, you have not been on an evening stroll with me for a long time. And neither have you told me any new stories lately."

"Don't worry. I will tell you lots of new and exciting tales again. I felt it was my responsibility to teach the local language to these uneducated, foreign labourers."

"Papa, you are putting in so much effort to teach them. Usually, to receive an education, students go to the teacher. But in this case, it's all TOPSY-TURVY. The teacher never chases the students to provide them with education. You, too, have been suffering in the bargain."

Gandhi, the humble teacher

Hearing this, Aisha's father chuckled and said, "From your perspective, you are right. But listening to you, I am reminded of this interesting story about Mahatma Gandhi."

"Which story, Papa?"

"Let me tell you. Mahatma Gandhi visited South Africa as a lawyer. As soon as he reached, he was disappointed at seeing the miserable situation of his fellow countrymen. Most Indian employees were not acquainted with the English."

"Due to that, they had to suffer consequences while trying to make a living in that foreign land. Even though Gandhi believed that every citizen should be well-versed in their native language, he realised that to live in a foreign country, knowledge of the English language was a must."

"So, he declared he would teach English to all the Indians who wished to learn it. He kept on waiting for people to come to him. During a prolonged wait of several weeks, just one office employee visited him to learn."

"Within the next few days, a salon worker and a shopkeeper also joined them. Each of them wanted just a basic working knowledge of English, so they could carry out their daily activities."

"Gandhi taught them the language, but because of their office jobs, they were not able to attend his classes regularly."

"Once, Gandhi waited for his students for hours, but none of them turned up. They were occupied with their jobs throughout the day. Finding no alternative, Gandhi started to visit them one by one to give them lessons."

"He became a translator for the customers of the salon worker."

"For the shopkeeper, he would translate product details into English. Often, he would help him with his day's accounts before leaving his shop."

"After much effort, Gandhi was able to teach the basics of the English language to his three students. He didn't receive any form of fees for his teaching. Besides, he had to put a lot of effort into his teaching."

"But after seeing his hard work bear fruit, he was *JOYFUl*. To become a great man, he had to focus his work in the direction where it was needed at the time, so his efforts could contribute to the world. Later on, he came to be known as the **FATHER OF THE NATION**."

Aisha listened to this tale about Gandhi with attention and interest. After a moment, she said, "Truly, Bapu was a great, great man!"

"Yes. Even I try my best to walk in his FOOTSTEPS. It is only by offering my contribution in these small ways that I feel my life's purpose is FULFILLING."

Hearing her father's words, Aisha felt very PROUD of him.

Following this, while still walking they came across the labourers working across the street.

They greeted their Masterji in the local language. Seeing this, Aisha was **DELIGHTED**.

By then, she was determined that she would try to **CONTRIBUTE** to the world, just like her father!

Gandhi In Noakhali

By Priya Mirza

During the last years of his life, Gandhi was a thin, frail man. But he was resilient—he had inner **strength**, and he saw himself as a *WARRIOR*. In 1916, Gandhi spoke about what it meant to be a warrior: a person fighting a real battle with themselves and facing difficult circumstances. A warrior accepts fighting as part of their life and is aware they are willingly moving closer to death. We all live and we all die, but how we die is the question.

Hatred and animosity

In 1946, India was finally drafting her constitution, making her own rules and becoming **independent** from the British. Indian freedom fighters such as Jawaharlal Nehru, Sardar Patel, and Maulana Azad were in New Delhi negotiating the terms of freedom with the British, but Gandhi wasn't there.

As the year was coming to an end, the Muslim League was, more than ever, determined that Pakistan be formed. Their leader, Muhammad Ali Jinnah, was adamant the League would not support Congress in any way. Gandhi was 77 that year and around him, the world he had believed in was giving way to a new one. His party also seemed eager to grasp power rather than consider the costs of independence for the

Gandhi on his way to Noakhali

citizens.

Gandhi did not want India to be PARTITIONED; he did not believe in the creation of a Muslim Pakistan because he did not think religion defined a person's identity completely. For Gandhi, the idea that Hindus and Muslims didn't want to coexist went against his beliefs. For hundreds of years, Hindus and Muslims had been living in this country, and Gandhi's idea of India was one inhabited by many people. He thought partition was an idea of politicians and leading communal parties like the Muslim League and the Hindu Mahasabha. Gandhi wanted to know what the citizens thought, and wanted a plebiscite held, where people would be asked if they wanted to create a state in the name of religion.

The costs of communalism

On August 16, 1946—known as Direct Action Day—Jinnah put out a call to all Muslims to stop doing businesses across

A refugee train on its way to Punjab, Pakistan, 1947

India. Jinnah wanted to pressure the British government into agreeing to create a Muslim-dominated country: Pakistan.

People all over attacked each other in the name of RELIGION. When the riots broke out in Noakhali, Gandhi chose to go there. But why Noakhali? It was a Muslim-dominated province in West Bengal (now in Bangladesh), and the people there had suffered terribly during the Bengal famine of 1943.

During World War II, the province was threatened by the attacks of the Japanese. Thousands had been displaced, and life wasn't easy. During this period, Huseyn Shaheed Suhrawardy, a Muslim League leader, came to power, and it was clear he would try his best to prove that Muslims could not live alongside Hindus.

The riots in Noakhali were brutal. Gandhi chose to go to Noakhali just to be with the wounded and grieving. Gandhi stayed, not discussing the Indian National Congress or the Muslim League, but simply talking to people. He calmly and fearlessly walked into an area where people had been killed

Destroyed house in Noakhali, 1946

and blood was on the streets aware that he, too, might be attacked. But he walked on.

During his stay in Noakhali, someone suggested punishing those who killed was the right thing to do. When **riots** break out people are scared, and in that fear, more **VIOLENCE** takes place. Gandhi knew retaliation creates an endless cycle of violence. The answer to violence is not violence, but **HEALING**.

Waging a war

When Gandhi arrived, people were **SUSPICIOUS** that this was part of the Congress' political activity. But Gandhi wasn't here for any political party: he was there because he loved his people. He was there to be part of the suffering and aid in healing. He held meetings, recited from the **QURAN**, sang **BHAJANS**, and helped people address the trauma. It wasn't easy: people were hostile and mean. The ruling party of West Bengal tried to malign his

Gandhi in Noakhali

presence there. Gandhi wanted to hold and comfort the people affected by the violence.

He stayed for more than four months, assuring people that TOGETHERNESS was possible. He was a gentle balm on the souls of all those who had lost loved ones. This sent a powerful message to the whole country.

Partition

And when Partition did come, it was horrific. Sometimes we think of Partition as one event, but it stretched over many years, and even today, people remember the horrors of that violence. Children were lost, women and men were thrown off trains and could never find their way home. When someone gets hurt, they remember the pain for a long time— forever, if the wound runs deep. Many years later, some are still struggling to locate lost families, thinking of the many people who died.

To Gandhi, this violence could happen because religion was seen as the only **principal** value of everyday life. But there is much more to our lives than that. We wake up, we look at the world surrounding us, we speak to each other, we meet our friends. We can do this even if we belong to different religions.

Our Constitution was drafted amidst BLOODSHED in New Delhi. There was so much violence that all leaders needed special passes to travel in the city. Gandhi himself was killed by a Hindu who felt Gandhi was more biased towards Muslims. More than ever, we need to remember all that mattered is that humans were killed. Everyone **suffered**—neither Pakistan nor India is free from that **TRAUMA** and **FEAR** Partition created, and **healing** and **LOVE** are the only way forward. Gandhi taught this not only to us but to the whole world.

Hidden Picture

**Gandhi Jayanti is celebrated on October 2. A statue of
Gandhiji is placed in one part of a museum. Find 10 of his
iconic glasses that are hidden in the museum.**

84

The Struggle

THOSE WHO ENSURED
INDIA WOKE UP TO HER FREEDOM
AT THE STROKE OF MIDNIGHT.

Odd One Out

August 9 is celebrated as Kranti Diwas. From each row, circle the freedom fighter who participated in the Quit India Movement of 1942.

Rani Laxmibai   Bahadur Shah Zafar   Mangal Pandey   Sardar Vallabhbhai Patel

Udham Singh   Annie Besant   Subhash Chandra Bose   Ram Prasad Bismil

Jawaharlal Nehru   Dadabhai Naoroji   Tatya Tope   Sukhdev Thapar

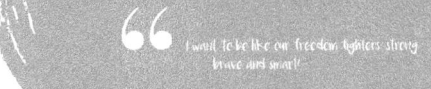
The Freedom Struggle

By Smita Dhruv

When Rohan returned from school, he was very excited. He had been selected to sing patriotic songs along with the National Anthem for the Independence Day celebrations at school that were going to be held on August 15.

As Rohan got down from the school bus and entered his colony, Anand Kutir Homes, he saw his neighbour, Aunty Nupur, writing something on the society board. She had a collection of old photographs with her.

"Hello, aunty," greeted Rohan, "I am selected for SINGING at the Independence Day celebrations in school next week!" he added excitedly.

"Rohan, that's wonderful news! I can help you practice!" offered Aunty Nupur.

Everyone knew Aunty Nupur to be helpful and knowledgeable. "Sure, thank you aunty," said Rohan and went home.

Since both his parents were working, Rohan was used to tidying up by himself.

He put the school bag and shoes in their proper place, washed his hands, feet and face with soap, changed his uniform, and ate the DELICIOUS snacks prepared by their helper Leela with a hot cup of milk.

After finishing his homework, he came out to play and saw Aunty Nupur still writing and sticking photographs on the society board.

"Aunty, who are these PHOTOGRAPHS of? Is this Gandhiji?" he asked looking at one of them.

"Yes, Rohan. This is a photograph of Mahatma Gandhi," Aunty Nupur replied.

The Quit India Movement

"Are you putting these up for the Independence Day celebrations? But there's no celebration here. This photo shows Gandhiji in jail!" said Rohan.

"Rohan, some of these photos are of a movement called QUIT INDIA in which Mahatma Gandhi asked the British to leave India. India's independence was achieved after a long war with the British Government. This war was not fought with guns and weapons, but with truth and non-violence."

"Satyagraha meant truth and Ahimsa was the non-violent way of achieving freedom. Many Indians participated like Jawaharlal Nehru, Sardar Patel, Maulana Azad and many

others whose names we do not know. They all followed Mahatma Gandhi's principles."

By then, Rohan's friends Sheel, Anju, Brij, Sukun and Mitesh had joined them and were listening to Aunty Nupur.

"How can one fight without weapons? That too against a strong ruler like the British?" asked Rohan.

"Yes, it was a difficult fight and required the strength of our leaders, who fought on the principles of truth and non-violence."

"In 1942, Mahatma Gandhi led the **PROTEST** under the All India Congress Committee (AICC) in Mumbai known as the Quit India Movement and demanded an end to the British rule in India. Interestingly, since the movement was held in the month of August it came to be known as **AUGUST KRANTI.** The movement started on August 9, 1942, and that day is celebrated as August KRANTI DIWAS. On this day, we remember our freedom fighters," Aunty Nupur explained.

Anju asked, "But Aunty, Independence Day was on August 15, 1947!"

Aunty Nupur replied, "Anju, the Quit India Movement did not result in the British leaving India immediately. When Gandhiji gave the slogan 'DO OR DIE' to the nation, it meant every Indian should participate in the protest, or die while protesting. Within hours of his speech, the members of the Indian National Congress were imprisoned without trial. It was declared an unlawful association. As a punishment, all its offices in the country were raided and its funds were frozen."

Mrs Lagate, another neighbour, also joined in and said, "I recall this story, Nupur. Initially, Quit India Movement was a peaceful protest, which later turned violent because of the reactions of the people. The arrest of Gandhiji and the Congress leaders led to **MASS DEMONSTRATIONS** throughout India. Thousands were killed and injured. Strikes were called in many places. The British tried to suppress the demonstrations and more than 1,00,000 people were imprisoned."

"Yes, Rima, I am glad that you remember it so well. Lord Linlithgow, the viceroy of India, adopted a policy of violence against people. The Quit India Movement united the Indians against the British rule. Although most demonstrations had been suppressed by 1944, when Gandhiji was released, he continued his resistance and went on a 21-day fast."

After the end of World War II in 1945, Britain's position had changed dramatically and the British Government could not ignore India's demand for independence. India finally achieved her freedom on the midnight of August 15, 1947," said Aunty Nupur.

An Independent India

Mrs Nair had something to add, "But look at the situation in Independent India today. We are ruling ourselves, but still have problems. People have many complaints against the government. There are issues that the government should deal with, one of them being unemployment."

This information surprised all the children. Brij asked, "Aunty, UNEMPLOYMENT means a person without job or earnings?"

Mrs Nair replied, "That is correct, Brij. Though a large percentage of our youth is educated, not many have jobs."

She added, "The government needs to discuss and take people in confidence on important issues. Otherwise, the unemployed people who are not happy with the government may have to go on strikes and processions, which were a common feature before Independence."

Aunty Nupur was pleased to see everyone participating in India's current issues.

She thought and wrote on the society board, "A presentation on India's current issues by the children of Anand Kutir Homes on August 15."

When children read this, they were all excited and decided to look up India's current problems and discuss them with their society members while celebrating Independence day.

Solve It

On this year, on August 15, India celebrates 75 years of Independence. There were many heroes and heroic acts that led to our freedom. Can you match the freedom fighters to their heroic acts?

(A) Bhikaiji Cama

(B) Rabindranath Tagore

(C) Subhas Chandra Bose

(D) Sarojini Naidu

(E) Bhagat Singh

(1) **Daily News** — Youth rebels bomb assembly

(2) **Daily News** — Indian Leaders Jailed for Civil Disobedience: 200,000 in protest

(3) **Daily News** — Poet gives up knighthood to protest the Jallianwala Bagh Massacre

(4) **Daily News** — Indian National Army launches attack on British Forces in Kohima

(5) **Daily News** — Indian flag unfurled on foreign soil for the first time

94

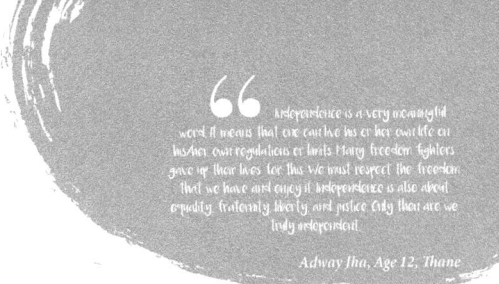
Bardoli

By Kumud Kumar

"Meghna, where are you going?" asked Tapti.

"Where else, Didi? I'm going to join the peasant movement at Bardoli," replied Meghna.

"I want to go there, too. I have heard that Sardar Patel is coming there today."

"Yes, hurry up. The women of the village have gone ahead."

Tapti and Meghna climbed a **BULLOCK** cart along with several others who were marching towards Bardoli, a small village near Surat in present day Gujarat. In the crowd, some people

playing the dholak and singing folk songs.

Sanju, a child sitting in the bullock cart, asked, "Tapti ben, why is everyone going to Bardoli?"

"Two years ago in 1926, the British government increased the agricultural tax levied on us farmers by 30 per cent. After we protested, the increased tax was reduced to 22 per cent. But we as farmers are facing difficult times. Floods are destroying our fields and we are starving. How will we pay the government?"

"So, why is everyone gathering at Bardoli?"

"We are all going to Bardoli to protest against this increased tax. Since 1922, freedom fighters have been conducting meetings here. Vallabhbhai Patel is coming to join the farmers' fight and we are all going there to support him."

A young freedom fighter

"Who is Vallabhbhai Patel?" Sanju asked.

"You haven't heard his name! His full name is Vallabhbhai Patel and he is a freedom fighter. He was the mayor of Ahmedabad but at the request of Mahatma Gandhi, he left and came to Bardoli to fight for the farmers."

Soon they reached the protest grounds in Bardoli. Sanju saw all the farmers sitting in rows, like disciplined soldiers. It was crowded. There were more women than men at the gathering.

Then Vallabhbhai Patel stepped onto the stage and said, "My dear brothers, I would like to warn you that if you oppose the British government, your problems will increase many times. They can and will snatch your land and property and take away every single grain you grow. Tell me, do you still want to confront them to reduce the increased taxes?"

"We're all ready for it. We would rather die than accept this injustice," said the crowd.

"Then you have already won this battle," replied Patel.

The following day, he along with the farmers wrote a letter to the Governor of Bombay Province, Sir Leslie Wilson, that increasing the taxes was a big MISTAKE. He demanded to set up an inquiry committee to conduct a fair investigation into the matter. He also stated that if no action was taken, the FARMERS WOULD NOT PAY THE

RENT, irrespective of the outcome.

But this letter had no effect on Wilson. On the contrary, he issued orders to his officers to strictly collect the taxes.

On February 12, 1928, Patel came to Bardoli and informed the farmers of the government's plan.

"What to do then? We have full faith in you. We will do what you say," the farmers said.

Patel replied, "We have to act courageously. We will not pay even a single penny until the government sets up an inquiry committee."

"We're all ready for it. None of us will pay a single penny," said the farmers.

Thus, the Bardoli Satyagraha started. To make it successful, Patel called in the support of other freedom fighters like Abbas Tayyab, Mumbai Legislative Council member KM Munshi and Constitutionalist Sir Tej Bahadur Sapru. Women actively participated in the movement. This movement got the full cooperation and support of Mahatma Gandhi.

The start of an era

Patel divided the Bardoli village into 13 activist camps for Satyagraha or Truth force.

An experienced leader was appointed to run each camp. Everyone worked day and night to put pressure on the British government to cut back the taxes. Gujarati publications like *The Patrika* published articles on the Satyagraha movement.

A team of spies was appointed which kept an eye on the government officers as well as protected those farmers who were being threatened to pay taxes.

Some farmers were threatened by the British officers. They oppressed the farmers and confiscated their property. Their cattle, grain, and even their household items were carried away in their own bullock carts.

Some farmers approached Patel and said, "If you permit, we can stop the British officers from coming into the villages. We can put barricades and HAMMER NAILS under the tyres of their vehicles so that they can't come here."

But Patel thought about it and said, "Our fight is not for a few thousand rupees. Our fight is a fight for principles. We are fighting for our SELF-ESTEEM and RIGHTS. This fight leads us to independence. We need the freedom to work and feed ourselves and our children."

"What do we do then?" asked the farmers.

"Separate the parts of your bullock carts. Untie the wheels and set them aside. If they can't carry your belongings on your bullock carts, they won't take much away."

The farmers liked the idea. But the oppression went on. Some farmers had no water to drink. Their troubles increased.

On the other hand, Gandhi was constantly writing against the attitude of the British government.

Gandhi declared a strike on June 12, 1928, to honour the Bardoli protest. He traveled to Bardoli to boost the courage of the farmers.

Many Indian members of the Legislative Council submitted their resignations to the Governor to raise awareness on the Bardoli satyagraha.

Lord Irwin, the Viceroy of India, was troubled by the news of the Satyagraha. He called Governor Wilson to Shimla on July 13, 1928 and said, "Mr. Wilson, the farmers' matter should be resolved at the earliest. We are being defamed in India and London."

After returning from Shimla, Wilson called Vallabhbhai Patel, Abbas Tyeb and other protestors for a discussion. He wanted to compromise with them. But they were not ready to settle for anything less than withdrawing the increased rates of agricultural taxes.

Fearing that the British government might arrest Patel at any time, Gandhi reached Bardoli on August 2. He announced, "If the government arrests Patel, I will lead this movement."

On hearing this, the British officers decided to conclude the movement. They didn't want the issue to be raised in the Parliament of England.

On August 6, 1928, they announced the release of all the arrested protestors and even returned their confiscated property and belongings. The increased amount of tax was being reduced to 6.03 per cent based on the decision of the inquiry committee.

The Bardoli Satyagraha opened the path for the Salt Satyagraha.

Due to the success of the movement, the farmers gave the title of 'Sardar' to Vallabhbhai Patel.

Gandhi said, "The Bardoli struggle was non-violent and though not a fight to attain freedom, but it brought us closer to freedom."

Hidden Picture

On August 8, Mahatma Gandhi launched the Quit India Movement to free India from the British rule. Our favourite Champakvan animals are re-enacting the movement for their school play and have lost 5 banners. Help them find the banners.

Right to Be Heard

By Soumitra Kanungo

Even today, protests are a way of voicing one's OPINIONS and they are a part of Indian history. India gained freedom because of protests.

As recently as in June 2020, the government of India passed three new farm bills that faced OPPOSITION from farmers across the country. Lakhs of farmers sat in protest on the outskirts of Delhi since the last week of November 2020, in the bitter cold, asking the government to roll back the bills that were passed without consulting them.

We asked some children what they thought about the farmers protests

Karishma Rathore, 12-year-old from Delhi says, "Farmers **WORK HARD** day and night to grow crops and feed the country. **The government should listen** to what they have to say."

Avisha Srivastava, 11-year-old from Indore, says, "The most remarkable feature of this **AGITATION** is the **UNITY** among the protesting farmers. It is noteworthy how the entire campaign has been organised while taking care of the basic needs of farmers. The worst thing surrounding this protest is the mistrust and anger of the farmers against the government and that they have gathered in large numbers during the times of coronavirus, which is a challenge for them."

Farmers carried food and water with them and have also received support from individuals and organisations who have been donating food to them.

However, the protest hasn't been easy. 12-year-old, Suhana Sharma from New Delhi says, "The farmers look tired and are living outside on the road. It is so SAD to see them. I asked my dad and he told me that they want the government to withdraw the three bills that were passed recently as they are not beneficial for farmers. If certain bills are made for farmers, the opinion of farmers should also be considered. I hope they win as they are responsible for feeding the country and we should do right by them."

The government had invited the representatives of the farmer organisations to discuss the matter. During the lunch break when food was offered to the farmers, they refused to eat and carried their own food in protest of the bills. According to the farmers, they didn't want to eat the food offered by the government officials as they have passed the bills and prevented farmers from cultivating food.

Know Your Rights

November 26 is Constitution Day in India. It celebrates the adoption of the Constitution of India. The constitution is a set of rights, rules and laws that we follow. Look at the pictures below and identify the actual rights we have as citizens of our country.

Right to stay out late at night.

Right to a clean environment.

Right to eat junk food.

Right to education.

Right to freedom of speech.

Right to be rude.

Right to equality.

Right to proper medical care.

Right to be heard.

Young Bhagat's Pledge

By Kusum Agarwal

Long before India attained independence from the British rule, Bhagat Singh was born to Sardar Kishan Singh, his wife Vidyawati in 1907, in Banga village in the Lyallpur district of Punjab. When Bhagat Singh was about 10 years old, Sardar Kishan Singh would often take him to the fields along with him.

While Kishan Singh scattered WhEat and MAIZE seeds on the land, Bhagat planted straws in the little mountains of soil that he made.

A new type of crop

One day, one of his father's friends, Nand Kishore noticed him 'planting'.

"Son, what are you doing?" asked Nand Kishore.

"I am sowing guns in my fields, uncle," replied Bhagat.

Bhagat's response astonished Nand Kishore.

"But son, these will grow into a lot of guns! What will you do with so many guns?" asked Nand Kishore.

"These guns will help me **FIGHT THE BRITISH** and help us get independence," replied Bhagat.

Nand Kishore was taken aback by Bhagat's answer!

He turned to his friend Kishan Singh and said, "Friend, your son is **courageous** and fearless. He will definitely make you proud one day!"

"Yes, he is quite different from other boys his age. He plays strange games with his friends. He divides them into groups and practices war tactics with them," said Kishan Singh.

Time flew by. Bhagat was now 12 years old and had started going to school.

An unforgettable tragedy

April 13, 1919 was Baisakhi and Bhagat was in class when he heard a disturbing news that made him leave his classroom quietly. He left for Amritsar on foot.

After walking 12 miles up and down from Amritsar, he returned home sad and upset.

"Son, come and have some food," his mother Vidyawati requested him. Sardar Kishan Singh too had returned home from the fields.

"Bhagat has not eaten anything. I have been calling him but he is not coming out of his room. He is very upset. Please ask him what is wrong!" said Vidyawati worriedly to her husband.

Kishan Singh went to Bhagat's room. He was surprised to see his brave son's face in tears!

"What is it, Bhagat? Please tell me why you are so sad," asked Kishan Singh.

Hearing his father's kind words, Bhagat hugged him and wept. "Father, I went to Amritsar today after I heard the news about the Jallianwala Bagh Massacre. I could not stop myself when I heard about the tragedy. I witnessed human massacre with my own EYES," he cried.

He then showed his father a box that contained blood-soaked soil of Jallianwala Bagh.

"Father, I vow on this soil today that I will not sit in peace till the day I get independence from the British rule," said Bhagat and made a pledge.

Kishan Singh was overwhelmed! He gave Bhagat a tight hug.

"Son, what you have just pledged at this young age is something even adults find difficult to commit to. You are a true patriot!" he said.

The young boy Bhagat grew up to become Shahid Bhagat Singh. He joined the freedom struggle and fought the British. Though he used violence, that Mahatma Gandhi did not approve of, he was a courageous freedom fighter. He and his two friends - Sukhdev and Rajguru, were hanged till death on March 23, 1931 in a prison in Lahore, a part of India then, for killing a British officer.

Dot to dot

Join the dots to find out who is celebrating Independence Day.

The Front-Bencher

By Kusum Agarwal

One morning, during the early 1900s, in pre-independent India, two brothers were getting ready to go to school. They lived in the city of Cuttack, Orissa, along with their large family.

"Brother, it's time to go to school.

Let's leave now," said Subhas to his elder brother, Sharad.

"What's the hurry? There's still time," responded Sharad casually.

"You don't understand. I want to go to school early today because I want to sit on the first bench. I always end up sitting behind. I think it's because I reach late," explained Subhas.

"In that case, let's leave right away!" said Sharad. The brothers left for school at once.

Subhas reached school earlier than usual and quickly occupied the front bench, which was still vacant. After a while, a British boy came in and asked him to vacate the seat.

"I won't get up from here. I came early today and was the first to sit here," said Subhas.

The disappointing realisation

The boy complained to the teacher who in turn asked Subhas to vacate the front bench. The teacher told Subhas that he was not allowed to sit there. Subhas felt dejected and moved to another bench at the back of the class.

That evening, on their way back home, Subhas asked his brother, "Why aren't we **ALLOWED** to sit on the front benches?"

Sharad did not know how to explain to his little brother that under the British rule, this is how Indian students were treated in a MISSIONARY SCHOOL.

Though Subhas was a bright student and scored the highest marks in his class, the scholarship was awarded to a British student. This again left Subhas heartbroken.

"We shouldn't study in this school anymore. If they discriminate amongst students this way, is it a school worth studying in?" Subhas asked his brother.

Again, Sharad had no reply.

After a few years, Subhas passed the matriculation examinations with a good score and secured an admission into the Presidency College in Kolkata. His father, Janki Das who was a well-known lawyer, and his mother, Prabhavati were overjoyed. They were certain that Subhas would make them proud.

One day, Subhas returned home from college quite upset.

"What's the matter, Subhas? You look gloomy today," said his mother, sensing something amiss.

"They expelled me from college," said Subhas sadly.

"But why? You were specially invited to study in that college by the principal himself. Why would he do that?" asked his mother shocked.

"One of our professors, Mr. Otten holds DISCRIMINATORY views about our country. So, when he said something disrespectful about India, and insulted some Indian students, I protested. And in the spur of the moment, I raised my hand, too. Therefore, they expelled me," explained Subhas.

His mother was apprehensive for a moment, but then she smiled.

A real patriot

"Subhas, how could you have sat quietly and listened to insults against

your own country? With regards to college decorum and discipline, what you did was wrong. But when seen from the point of view of UPHOLDING the RESPECT of your country, you did the RIGHT THING. The notion of freedom runs in your veins. I am proud of you, son," said his mother.

"Thank you, mother," said Subhas, who felt much better now.

His mother hugged him and said, "Our country won't be under the British rule for long because of people like you who stand up for their country."

That boy grew up to be Netaji Subhas Chandra Bose, one of the most prominent freedom fighters of our country.

Subhas Chandra Bose set up the AZAD HIND FAUJ, an army he raised with the help of the German government to wage war against Britain. He was also the first person to address Mahatma Gandhi as the Father of the Nation in a speech delivered on 6 July 1944, through the Azad Hind Radio from Singapore.

His slogan, "GIVE ME BLOOD, AND I SHALL GIVE YOU FREEDOM" went a long way in uniting the citizens of India against the British rule.

Dot to dot

Join the dots to find out who is the father of the Indian Constitution.

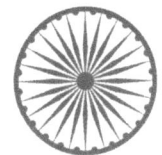

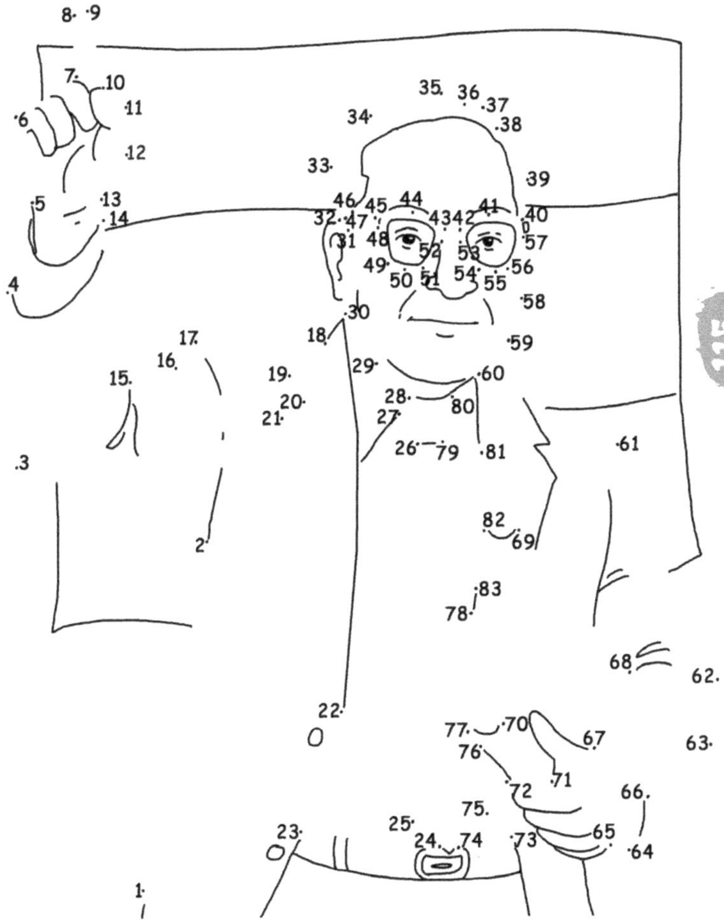

An Untouchable Tale

By Kumud Kumar

Before India's independence, caste discrimination and **untouchability** were practiced in Hindu society. There were many who suffered because of this. One of those who suffered was Dr. Bhimrao Ambedkar, who later went on to become the Father of the Indian Constitution.

Discrimination against untouchables

During his childhood, Bhimrao was travelling by train with his elder brother to meet his father, Ramji Sakpal. The two brothers got off at a small station called Masur in Maharashtra.

Their father lived far away from the station, so Bhimrao and his brother decided to hire a hand-pulled **RICKSHAW**, which was common during those days.

The rickshaw-puller made them sit in his rickshaw and started pulling it. He chatted with the two boys and after some distance, asked, "Children, what is your caste?"

"We are Mahars," said the boys.

The rickshaw-puller was very **ANGRY** and gave the rickshaw a violent jerk and both the boys fell off.

The rickshaw-puller began shouting at the boys. "How dare you sit in my rickshaw! You have now polluted my rickshaw!"

A CROWD gathered there and more people came as news spread that two Mahar children had sat in the rickshaw and made it UNHOLY for the upper caste.

"What can you expect from such low-caste children?" said someone.

"These untouchables have not only polluted the rickshaw, they have ruined the poor man's day," said someone else.

Bhimrao and his brother did not know what to do. No one took their side. All they were told again and again was that being born in a lower caste was a sin.

They began getting scared, when the rickshaw-puller began abusing them. After a long time, the crowd moved away and the boys were left alone.

They had no choice now, but to WALK to their father's house. It was hot and DUSTY. As they walked, the boys

began to feel thirsty and tired. But nobody offered them water.

They could not drink water from a well or from the lake as in those days, lower castes were not allowed to touch wells or lakes.

People thought even their touch would pollute the water bodies. So, unless someone poured water for them to drink, the boys had to remain without water.

Cruel Treatment

But since they were so thirsty, Bhimrao forgot all about his caste, drew water from a well and started drinking it.

But before he could drink enough, he heard someone SCREAMING.

The well belonged to the high castes and someone from that caste had seen them drinking water from the well. The bucket and the well both had now become dirty.

Soon, a crowd gathered because of the shouting.

Bhimrao felt he was surrounded by a pack of wolves ready to pounce and eat them up.

The crowd then started discussing how they could recover the cost of the damage done by the boys.

The people began beating the boys. Nobody stopped to think that these were two thirsty children. All that they had done was drank some water, which was a gift of nature. But to the crowd, the boys were low caste and deserved to be beaten.

Some in the crowd began saying that beating the boys was not enough. They had to be punished even more severely.

They decided to shave the boys' heads and some people ran to look for a barber. But in those days, it was difficult to find a barber who would shave the head of a lower caste person!

None of the barbers in Masur agreed to shave the boys' heads.

The barbers were **SCARED** that no one would come to them if they knew that they had touched a lower caste boy.

The two brothers were beaten up badly, and finally managed to escape the angry crowd.

This incident affected Bhimrao deeply. He started thinking about ways to remove the caste system from Indian society.

He realised that education was the only way to free himself and others like him from such horrible injustice.

Bhimrao became a scholar. He became a doctor in 1927 from Columbia University in New York City for his thesis 'National Dividend of India—A Historic and Analytical Study'.

In 1923, he went for further education in Economics from London School of Economics.

Bhimrao Ambedkar not only drafted the Constitution of India, but he was also India's first Law Minister.

To make people aware about how badly lower castes were treated in India, he took part in several revolutions, wrote many books, and edited newspapers.

It was on the principle of equality and friendship, he wanted a new India to emerge from the British rule.

Unfortunately even today, lower caste Indians DO NOT GET TREATED EQUALLY. In upper caste houses, they are not allowed to sit on chairs, have to eat from a different plate and they still get badly treated in many other ways as if they are lesser.

A Pledge

CELEBRATING INDIA
THROUGH ITS FESTIVALS.

Solve It

Several harvest festivals are celebrated in March and April. These also mark the beginning of a new year. Match the festivals to the states they belong.

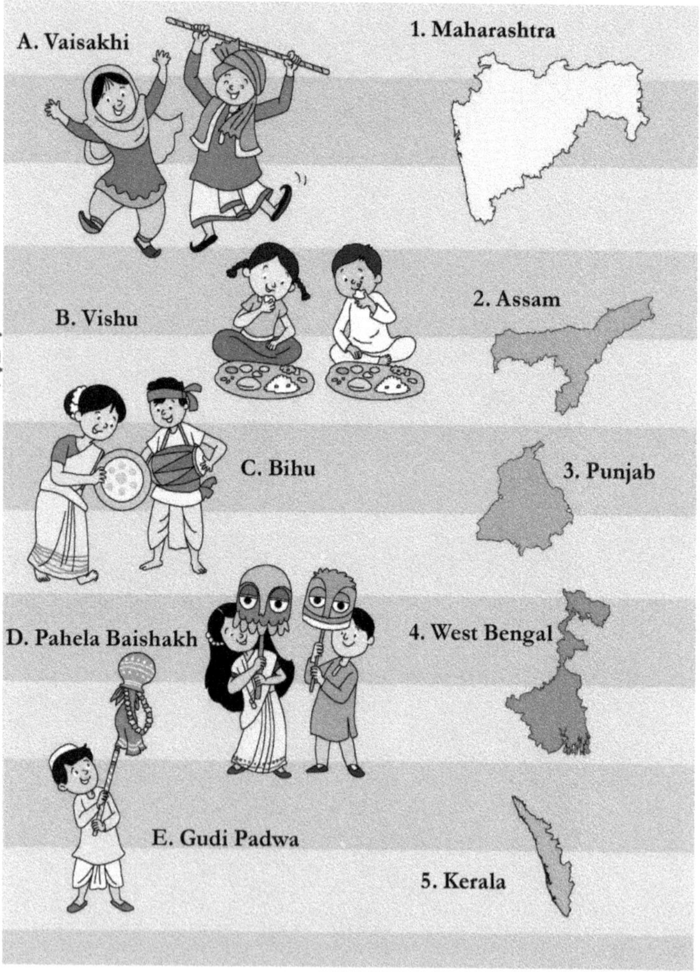

A. Vaisakhi

1. Maharashtra

B. Vishu

2. Assam

C. Bihu

3. Punjab

D. Pahela Baishakh

4. West Bengal

E. Gudi Padwa

5. Kerala

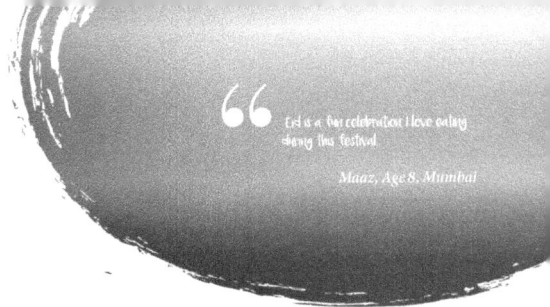
Eid Mubarak!

Abdul hid behind a pillar and watched his father get ready. Baba wore his cap, slipped on his sandals and headed towards the mosque. Abdul silently followed him. It was already past sunset. In the dark, everyone held their breath and waited for the moon to come. Soon, a thin crescent could be seen shining, hanging low in the eastern sky. Everyone said a prayer and hugged each other. Greetings of Eid Mubarak were heard all around. Celebrations had begun for EID-UL-FITR!

Abdul rushed home to tell the others. He loved Eid! He looked forward to meeting all his cousins. They all would parade around the house together, wearing their new clothes and looking like a bunch of noisy peacocks!

Eid Celebrations

Abdul couldn't wait for the festive feast, with mouth-watering dishes and delicious sweets! The aroma of spices from **biryani** and haleem, refreshing **DAHI VADAS**, creamy **SHEER KURMA**, the rich **shahi tukda** and qubbani ka meetha! But more than anything, Abdul enjoyed dining with his entire family—parents, grandparents, brothers, sisters, aunts, uncles and

cousins. They would sit together, talking to each other, passing food around and smiling lovingly. Abdul felt happy and blessed.

Amreen Fatema, who lives in Hyderabad, says that FOOD is her favourite part of Eid. 'During Ramadan, we wait eagerly for iftar. When we break our fast at sunset, we are given a variety of food. I look forward to eating haleem and dahi vadas. And on Eid, there are so many dishes!' she says. Her brother Ali, on the other hand, looks forward to receiving EIDI. 'It is money that the elders give youngsters and children on Eid. Some kids choose to save their eidi, but I prefer spending mine on things that I like,' he explains.

Dilip, who lives in Mangalore, also loves Eid because of food. 'Our neighbour, Qamrunnisa aunty, brings us a plate of special food on Eid. Sweets and snacks are put into beautiful white bowls, arranged on a plate and covered with a LACE cloth. It looks so tempting. And the sevaiyan that aunty makes is delicious!' he declares.

Every year, Muslims all over the world celebrate the festival of Eid-ul-Fitr at the end of the holy month of Ramadan. They pray, spend time with their families, meet and greet their friends and relatives, and have lots and lots of delicious food. What will you share during Eid this year?

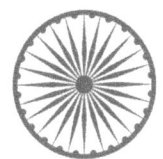

Hidden Picture

Razia and Rehman have hidden 13 bowls of kheer in their dining room. Find all the bowls of Kheer and start the Eid celebrations.

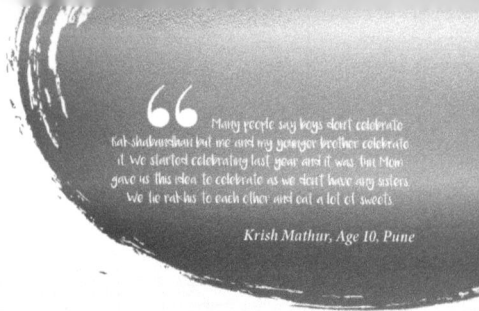
Hassan's Trip To Dawar

By Lekshmi Gopinathan

"Hassan," Ammi's voice pierced through the rhythmic whooshing winds.

Hassan looked up from his book. "Coming, Ammi!" He stood up and dusted his pyjamas.

He looked serious, like a child forced to grow before his years. He remembered running around and playing with his friends on the school playground as if it was yesterday.

It was Independence Day today, and for as long as Hassan could remember, it used to be a day of celebration, sport and sweets, but that felt like a distant memory.

Now all he could think of was the sound of marching feet and armed patrol jeeps that sent him into a self-created shell. Those sounds scared him, and he felt they were the reason for the humongous changes in his young life.

"What are you doing, my son?" Ammi asked lovingly as Hassan approached her.

"Reading this book for the tenth time, Ammi," Hassan responded and with a smile, never too tired for his mother's questions.

The family decision

Abba had come home from the market after finishing odd jobs, as was now the norm. His face was flushed with excitement as he sat next to Ammi. Hassan had overheard his parents discuss moving from Srinagar over the past year, but wasn't sure if it would ever happen.

Over two years, Hassan had settled into a life that felt that was different from the childhood he had known. In the beginning, he used to slip out of the house occasionally and meet his friends. However, the coronavirus pandemic put a spoke in that wheel too.

Online classes over a broken internet and sometimes over community radio while Ammi and Abba took turns HOMESCHOOLING him were the routine.

Amir, his closest friend, had moved away with his parents to their village, and now it seemed like their turn.

"Hassan, we want to speak to you about the move," said Abba.

"Yes, Abba." Hassan dutifully sat next to his father.

"You know how tough times have been for us; we are moving to Dawar."

Hassan's face lit up as he faintly remembered Abba's village, though they hadn't been there in a while. All he

could remember was a gushing river, a pristine valley and beautiful tall mountains.

"How far is Dawar, Abba?"

"It's not very far, son, a little more than 100 kilometres from here."

"How will we get there, Abba? Where will we live? Can I go to a school there? Will you and Ammi have jobs there?" Hassan's questions left him breathless.

"Yes, life will be different there. It will be full of HOPE." Ammi planted a kiss on Hassan's forehead and pulled him into an embrace. Hassan slipped into Ammi's arms and smiled.

"Will I be able to go to a school there?" Ammi and Abba looked at each other.

"We will find a way for you to read and learn, Hassan. We promise."

"How will we go, Abba?"

"We will catch the first car out of Srinagar to Gurez Valley next Monday."

Hassan's mind was filled with DREAMS of a brighter tomorrow. The week flew by. Hassan was kept busy packing and saying goodbyes to friends and neighbours, all masked up, with no hugs but hearts full of love.

Ammi and Hassan made a dozen rakhis for Ammi to tie on all her friends' wrists who had been as close as siblings throughout her life in Srinagar.

This year, Rakshabandhan would be different, but the tradition would be kept alive.

"Why do you tie rakhis to your friends?"

"Because they have helped me, stood by my side and protected me all these years, especially through the tough times, just like siblings would."

Before they knew it, it was the day for the trip to Dawar. The evening before the trip, Ammi decided to cook Hassan's favourite, modur pulao. She cooked the rice while Hassan soaked the saffron in water as directed.

"Would you like to tie a rakhi on someone, Hassan?" Ammi asked as she heated ghee in a pan and added cloves, bay leaves, a cinnamon stick, cardamom, and peppercorns. Hassan chewed his upper lip and frowned, "I don't know, Ammi, all my friends have moved."

"That's okay. You will make new, meaningful relationships in the village. Take one from my bunch and tie it on the next new friend you make." Ammi cooked the sugar into a thick syrup.

Hassan ran to Ammi's room, got the rakhi, nodded to himself and folded it safely, placing it in his small bag pocket.

Ammi added the cooked rice to the pot and topped it with chopped dates, raisins, almonds and cashews.

Hassan poured the saffron water on the top, and his favourite meal was ready. The kitchen smelt of its last meal.

Unexpected encounter

The next morning, Hassan climbed into the car. He felt a dread of leaving the known and moving towards the unknown. Abba had mentioned that Dawar was shut from the mainland for many months during the winter because of heavy snow. That's why they had to wait until now for their move. Hassan sat pale-faced next to Ammi, with a lemon in his hand to combat motion sickness.

He had been expecting a short trip. Little did he know that

serpentine roads awaited, curvy and bumpy. Their heads banged against the roof a dozen times throughout the trip.

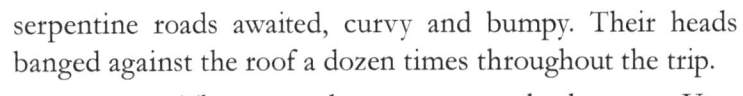

They passed many army check gates. Very soon, it started DRIZZLING, and the roads turned muddy in no time. The car ploughed through the slush.

The sound of thunder stopped the car in its tracks. A huge branch had fallen, obstructing their way.

Dark and gloomy, there was nothing optimistic about the weather. Passengers poured out to check what could be done. Hassan sat close to Ammi.

The sound of a truck pulled him out of his thoughts. He peeped out to see an army truck pull up close behind their car. A soldier rushed towards them.

Hassan was scared; all the fearful thoughts came rushing back. Were they in trouble? Would they get hurt? His eyes brimming with tears. Nothing felt right.

Before they knew it, half a dozen **soldiers** had jumped out of the truck and were helping move the fallen tree trunk out of the way.

A soldier's face appeared by the window, asking them to pull down the glass. "Are you all okay?" a kind voice asked them.

Ammi nodded and smiled as Hassan looked at him in fear. "What about you?"

Hassan felt like somebody broke his dam; he burst into tears.

The soldier opened the door and waited for Hassan to calm down. "What's your name?"

"Hassan."

"Why are you crying, Hassan? Is it because of the fallen tree?"

Hassan nodded. The soldier looked intrigued, "What is wrong then?"

"Everything."

The soldier smiled, got Ammi's permission and took Hassan out of the car. The rain had reduced to a trickle. The passengers and soldiers were still working on moving the trunk.

"So, Hassan, where are you headed?"

"Dawar, Sir."

"Dawar, that's a beautiful village."

"Have you been there, Sir?" Hassan's looked at him, wiping away his tears.

"Yes, I have, many a time. It's very close to the Line of Control. Do you know what the Line of Control is?"

Hassan nodded. He knew that the Line of Control or LOC divided the boundaries of India and Pakistan in Jammu and Kashmir.

"Would you like to know more about Dawar?"

Hassan nodded, sniffling. Why did the soldier sound so kind and sensitive? Were his assumptions wrong all along?

"The magnificent **KISHENGANGA** River flows through the village, flanked by mountains. For six months a year, the village is cut off from the world because of snow. The mountains are then capped with white. Now, during the summer, they will be speckled with green. The cottages are built of stone and wood, and the people there are very loving and kind."

"What do people do there, Sir?" Hassan was intrigued.

"They farm and grow their food. It's a close-knit community. Everyone supports the other, even in the cold winter months. Also, the army is always available for any urgent requirements all through the year."

"Where are you headed to, Sir? Are you coming to Dawar too?"

The soldier smiled, "No, Hassan, we are headed to Burnai, the last village, right before Chakwali, where the line divides India and Pakistan. In fact, in Dawar, you can view the mountains which stand in Pakistan, right from the Indian soil."

The tree had been cleared and everyone went into the car. The soldier decided to accompany Hassan and told him stories of Dawar as they drove to the village. He filled the journey with anecdotes and the car rang with laughter.

As they reached the village, the soldier said, "Hassan, I know the days have been tough. Especially for a small kid like you." Then, he turned away, refusing to let his emotions get in the way of their conversation. Wiping the side of his eye, he turned towards Hassan, "I had someone once who was as young as you, full of questions."

"Where is that person now, Sir"?

"Lost to war, like many innocent young children. It was a long time ago."

Hassan couldn't understand these words. "But, Hassan, there is always hope, and for you, there is an abundance of that. Never lose hope. Is there anything you want that I can help you with? Just ask."

Hassan smiled thoughtfully, gathered courage and burst out, "I want to study from a teacher, sir. I want to go back to my classes. Not on the phone, which has bad internet and not on the radio where I can't ask questions."

The soldier looked at him and then nodded. "I will make sure that you have books and a teacher who will come to give you lessons each week."

New friends

Hassan's heart skipped a beat. Was this really happening? Would he get a chance to learn again?

"We will make the **arrangements**." Hassan's joy knew no bounds. He jumped and hugged the soldier tight. "Ammi, can I give some modur *PULAO* to Sir?"

Ammi smiled and

gave the box to Hassan who handed it over to his new friend.

"This is for you, Sir. It's my favourite dish. Also, can I give you something else? Please show me your wrist."

The soldier extended his hand. Out came the rakhi from Hassan's bag, and he lovingly tied it around his new friend's wrist.

"We will always protect you, Hassan." The soldier smiled and patted his head.

He went back into his truck and Hassan's family walked ahead.

Hassan walked through the **MAIZE** fields, his hands touching the *WILDFLOWERS* sprouting in rebellion amid the crops. A faint smile crossed his face as the soft flowers touched his small palms.

Hassan picked up speed and raced towards the small cottage in view, where his new home and dreams awaited.

He was going to be able to learn again.

Map Quest

Onam is a festival celebrated in Kerala. Rano wants to participate in the Pookalam Rangoli competition. Help her choose the right group based on her preferences.

- Rano likes using maroon, orange and white flowers to make the pookalam rangoli.
- She doesn't like using purple flowers.
- She likes making flower-shaped rangolis.

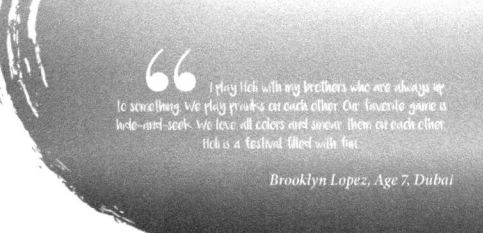
An Onam, With Love

By Lekshmi Gopinathan

The fragrance of flowers wafted through the air and blended with the smoky aroma of spluttering MUSTARD in the kitchen. Athira took a deep breath and pulled in a lungful of her favorite smells. Her eyes twinkled as she adorned her short, neatly combed hair with a single strand of JASMINE.

Everything felt different today, and while Athira and her grandmother had celebrated Onam as long as little Athira could remember from her seven years, this year was special.

As she raced to the kitchen, her eyes caught the beautiful pookalam—the magnificent flower arrangement at the entrance.

Onam celebration

For ten days leading to Onam, they had made different patterns, but today the pookalam looked perfect—even the flowers were singing along with her heart.

She reached the kitchen and caught her breath. Her grandmother picked up a handful of grated COCONUT and added it into a pan. The slow roasting along with the faint sound of coconut oil bubbling in the background where

JACKFRUIT chips floated merrily were a celebration for the senses.

Ammamma was dressed in a simple cream mundu and neriyathu, a two-piece clothing ensemble, which made her look lovelier than she already was.

She turned around and looked at Athira. "My dear child, you look beautiful."

Athira did a happy spin and her gold-rimmed kasavu skirt twirled along. "So do you, Ammamma." Athira loved the gentle smile on her grandmother's face.

"What are you making, Ammamma?" Athira jumped up and down. She had worked hard with Amma, Dad, and Ammamma to prep for the **Onam sadya**, an elaborate meal that the family made on this special day.

Grandma laughed. "Just adding the final touches to our sadya, Athira kutty. There are at least **25** dishes that will be served." Athira was always bewildered by the amount of food that went on the platter on Onam day.

Athira nodded jubilantly. Her heart fluttered thinking about the Onam sadya.

Boat race

"Ammamma, if we were in Kerala, what else would we be doing today?" Athira shifted her weight from one foot to the other, eager to hear her grandmother's tales.

Ammamma's eyes **twinkled** as they always did while narrating stories to Athira. "For one, we would go to Kuttanad and watch a Vallamkalli, the annual boat race that's held in various parts of Kerala on Onam. Families, clans, and sometimes even villages compete against each other during these races."

"Are these boats very fast, Ammamma?"

The boats aren't, but the racers are—they row so fast while being cheered on by their fans and friends. And these boats are specially made. They are called SERPENT boats."

"Wow, serpent boats?"

"Yes, long boats, which were once used as war boats and look like the hooded head of a snake."

"That would be so thrilling, wouldn't it? What else would we do, Ammamma?"

"We would also sing and dance. Remember when all of us sat together in a circle and did that two Onams ago?"

"Oh yes, Thumbi Thullal. I sang

with all of you and we had so much fun."

Ammamma swept Athira off her feet and embraced her. "Yes, it's always fun to get together with friends and families for a celebration. That's the spirit of Thiruvonam, our happy Onam."

Athira giggled in Ammamma's embrace.

She turned and looked at the kitchen and it felt like a scene right out of the cookbook. There was freshly made sambhar with a generous dollop of ghee, some lip-smacking puli inji, which was a combination of sweet and spicy ginger chutney, sharkara varrati, similar to banana chips dipped in wholesome jaggery, pineapple pachadi, a yummy yoghurt-based dish, the mouth-watering ada payasam, and so much more.

Athira switched on the family computer. Before the sadya all the cousins were going to join in a video call from all parts of the world. Though it wasn't even close to the camaraderie they shared in-person, it still felt good to know they were all together in spirit.

Ammamma and Athira cleaned five banana leaves and placed them on the floor along with seating mats.

"Why do we use banana leaves, Ammamma?"

"Because they are organic, chemical-free, add a special flavor to the food, and also end up holding all the food that no plate can." The room rang with laughter.

The dishes were all placed on the floor, ready to be served as soon as Amma and Dad arrived. Athira couldn't wait any longer. Her foot tapped impatiently on the floor as she glanced at the door every two minutes.

She looked at all the dishes and was wondering how they all fit the leaf so well, year after year.

She turned around and looked at the big fluffy papadams,

the olan with a generous dash of coconut milk, hand-strained over many hours, the humble but nutritious avial, a creamy mix of all vegetables available, topped with grated coconut. She could taste the ghee on the parippu, a gravy, and she could smell the tangy rasam, opening up her nostrils with the hint of pepper.

Wildlife conservation

"Ammamma, what's your favorite childhood experience for Onam?"

"Mine?" Ammamma frowned, thinking hard, and then her face lit up as she pulled a thought from her closet of memories.

"It has to be the one with pullikalli."

"Pullikalli? Tiger dance?" Athira vaguely remembered watching a documentary on it.

"Yes, my child. Artists would paint themselves to resemble TIGERS and dance enthusiastically. All the performers had decades of experience. I remember being in awe when I saw them first."

"Is that why you became a wildlife conservationist?" Athira's eyes were wide open. Ammamma was a well-known environment writer, having many books published to her name.

Ammamma smiled. "I have never thought of it that way. I always thought it was because of your grandfather's postings as Forest Officer and me being influenced by that all my life. But maybe you are right, maybe something did plant a seed in my heart, long before that."

The sound of the horn of her parents' car pulled her out of her thoughts.

Athira rushed to the door and peeped out. Her Amma with her kind open smile and her Dad with his hearty laughter were walking towards her and her Amma's hand held another small hand, four-year-old Kanav—her new brother.

Athira ran towards them and then stopped in her tracks: she had been advised to act calmly around Kanav until her adopted young brother felt comfortable in the new surroundings. But she didn't have to worry, because Kanav pulled his tiny hand away from Amma's and ran straight to Athira.

They had been playing together for weeks now, getting to know each other. Athira hugged her little brother tight, vowing to love and protect him.

Her eyes shining with tears, she looked at the eager face of Kanav.

"Come, Kanav, let me serve you Onam sadya and tell you all about pullikalli."

"What is that, chechi?" Kanav looked at his big sister with eyes full of curiosity.

"It's a story of how our Ammamma found what she loved."

Kanav jumped up and down, and they went to feast a belly full as their hearts brimmed.

Five beaming faces and a happy Onam, indeed.

"My dear child, you look beautiful."

"It's always fun to get together with friends and families for a celebration. That's the spirit of Thiruvonam, our happy Onam."

Artists would paint themselves to resemble tigers and dance enthusiastically.

Kanav pulled his tiny hand away from Amma's and ran straight to Athira.

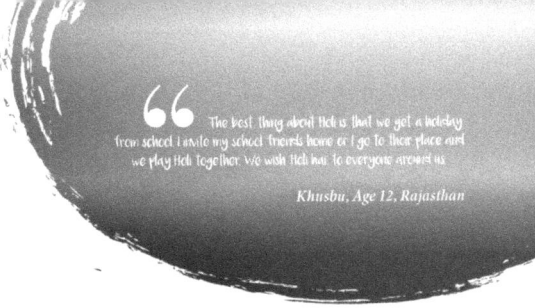

The Real Reason

By Medhavini Mohan

Julie was sad when she came home from school. After lunch, as was her habit, she didn't sit and talk to Ma about what happened in school that day. Instead, she ate and went to her room.

Ma waited for a little time, and when Julie did not come out, went to her room. She found Julie lying in bed, silent. "What happened, dear?" asked Ma, stroking Julie's hair.

Julie burst into tears and blurted, "The teacher has put me in the back row for the group dance. She does this every time!"

"So much crying for just this? Maybe the other children dance better," consoled Ma.

Unfair judgement

"No, ma. That's not the reason. I know why she put me in the last row!" said Julie, sobbing. "You know I love to dance, and I asked you to make me join Kathak dance classes. I have also been learning modern dance. You know that Ma."

"Yes dear. I know you have been practising very hard," said Ma.

"And when the auditions for the group dance were announced, I practised even more and I was selected. But Vidisha ma'am put me in the last row. Three girls who make so many dance mistakes are in the first row. Ma'am even asked me to teach them the steps," explained Julie.

"Oh. If she thinks you're so good, why did she not put you in the front row?" asked Ma.

"First, I thought it was because there was something wrong with my dance. But from the time I have started dancing in class 1 to now, I have never been put in front. This time, I worked so hard and I know I dance better than most others. But still, I'm in the last row," sobbed Julie.

"Why is that?" asked Ma.

"Because I'm **DARK**. That's why!" exclaimed Julie.

Ma hugged Julie. She now understood what Julie was going through. When Ma had been in school, she too had often been teased by others for being dark.

Ma did not want Julie to grow up feeling the same way, so she had brought her up to think that **good qualities** were more important than skin colour. But what could a child do when a teacher was being unfair?

"And in class, Vidisha ma'am is not so strict with children who are fair. Can you complain to the principal, Ma?" asked Julie, still talking.

Her mother

thought for a while. "Julie, I think there's another way to make your teacher understand. It may be difficult to prove that she is being unfair because of your skin COLOUR. Let me think," said ma.

Julie and Ma sat quietly for some time. Then Ma asked, "Julie, isn't Vidisha ma'am your language teacher? She has given you an essay to write on 'what I want to become', hasn't she?"

Thoughtful essay

"Yes, Ma. I will finish it today. We are supposed to read it out in class tomorrow. I'm going to write that I want to become a DANCER!"

"Well Julie, what if you write about how you want to be a TEACHER?" Ma laughed and looked at Julie with a twinkle in her eyes.

Julie understood what Ma meant! "Oh yes! Thank you for this idea, Ma!"

The next day, all the children had to read their essays in Vidisha ma'am's class. Soon, it was Julie's turn.

She picked up her notebook and started reading, "I want to become a teacher when I grow up because just one teacher can make or break the future of so many kids. It is a very IMPORTANT job. When I become a teacher, I will make sure that all children are treated **EQUALLY** in my class. I will pay attention to their talent and abilities, and not to the colour of their skin. I will not behave differently to a child who is dark or fair, tall or short.

I will not do anything to make any child feel sad. And just like my teachers here, I will put in all my effort to teach the children."

All the children in class who had been ignored because of their colour or size clapped loudly and cheered when Julie finished.

Vidisha ma'am understood what Julie had done. Without complaining or blaming anyone, she had said what she wanted to say.

That day, when dance practice began, Vidisha ma'am changed the order of dancers.

Julie was now in the front row, along with many **ACCOMPLISHED** dancers. Julie danced happily, like a bird who had been set free from the cage.

Colour Me

149

The Way Things Used to Be

By Susan Kneib Schank

Jihan heaved a bag of groceries into the car. "So much food for one meal!"

"I know. Imagine if we were having undhiyu, too," said Mom.

"We're not?" said Jihan.

"Aunt Anandi says it's too early for undhiyu. She'll make mixed vegetables with beans and potatoes. Like potato undhiyu," said Mom.

Jihan groaned. "Potato undhiyu?"

Mom smiled. "You might like it."

Nostalgic affair

Jihan didn't want to try potato undhiyu for Diwali at Aunt Anandi's house. He wanted things to be the way they used to be, at Grandma's (or Ba, as the family called her). Jihan would always help Ba cook the meal, and she'd tell him about Diwali when she was a girl. He'd laugh as she told about the time she

fell in the mud while picking soft clay for DIYAS.

That night, Mom and Jihan started preparing food for the next day's feast.

"Why don't you fold the ghoogras?" said Mom. "Ba always said you folded them best."

"I miss her so much!" Jihan said.

"I do, too," said Mom. "But she'd be happy to know we were cooking her favorite recipes, right?"

"I guess," said Jihan. *But what about Ba's undhiyu recipe?* he thought.

Mom chatted while they worked. Jihan stayed quiet.

"Will you tell me Ba's story about Diwali when she was a kid?" Jihan said before he went to bed.

Mom smiled. "You would tell it better. And I found something at Ba's that might help you." She left the room and came back with a small book.

Jihan read the note on the **JOURNAL**.

It said:

For Jihan, who loves stories as much as I do. Write what's in your heart. Love, Ba.

"She meant it for your birthday, but I think you need it early. Why don't you write her story in here?" said Mom.

Jihan opened the journal and stared at the blank page for a while. Then, he began to write.

A potato filled Diwali

"Happy Diwali!" Mom sang the next morning.

Jihan sat up. "Potato undhiyu. Yippee."

"We'll have lots to eat," Mom said.

Jihan got ready slowly. He was about to head downstairs when he saw the journal. He slipped it into his pocket.

Jihan's cousin, Aloka, answered the door. "You're here!" she cried. "We can't wait for you to try our potato undhiyu!"

"I can't wait either," Jihan said politely. "I keep thinking about it."

Jihan felt a lump in his throat when he saw the table being set with Ba's **copper** thali set. Soon, the family sat down. Food was passed. Plates were filled. Jihan looked at the potato undhiyu Aunt Anandi put on his plate. It didn't look like undhiyu. He took a small bite anyway and was surprised. "It's not bad," he said.

Aloka smiled. "Glad you like it."

Jihan looked around. It wasn't Ba's house, but it was family. He patted the journal in his pocket. "Hey, Aloka. Want to hear a story later?"

Jihan didn't want to try potato undhiyu at Aunt Anandi's house.

Find the Gifts

Chirstmas is celebrated on December 25. Santa's gift bag spilled when all the elves came to meet him before Christmas. Find the hidden toys.

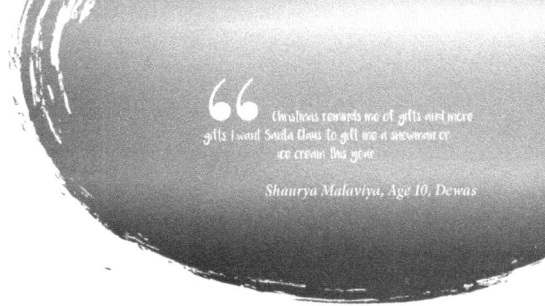
Bijoy's Christmas

By Niloy Kurmi

"You know what, Baideo, it is *gloomy* enough without an alien in the house," said Bijoy, as his elder sister, Mamta Baideo, sat down at the table for breakfast.

But Mamta did not seem to mind her green face pack, which made her look like an EXTRATERRESTRIAL. She had put it on last night as a remedy for the humongous pimple on her nose.

155

"Say whatever you like," huffed Mamta, "but with this apple growing on my nose, how can I possibly attend the virtual CHRISTMAS event organized by our college? So, I need to get rid of it as soon as possible!"

Bijoy did not reply but shot Mamta an angry look over his bowl of cornflakes. Mamta took no heed of it. She had become quite used to her brother's **SULKINESS** now. It had started last week—this bad mood of her brother's, which was mainly directed at her.

The sibling bond

Last Monday, Mamta had rocked the whole house, screaming. After waking up early that morning, she had gone to the bathroom.

When she saw her **reflection** in the mirror, she bolted out of her room, yelling at the top of her voice. And she did not stop screaming until their parents made Bijoy apologize for his rude behaviour.

"Why on earth, Bijoy, did you draw facial **HAIR** on Mamta's face while she was asleep?" asked Bijoy's parents. "Say sorry to your sister now!"

Mamta knew why her brother had been behaving this way. It was Christmas! And, like every year, he wanted a **PARTY**.

Throwing a party, however, was the most impractical thing to do in today's time, when the whole world was facing a deadly **PANDEMIC**.

And yet, Mamta had tried to lift Bijoy's spirits by making him a Christmas card.

But if even this can't cheer him up, what else can I do? thought Mamta. Small children can be very unreasonable sometimes; Mamta knew it.

Presently, she gave Bijoy a dirty look, as if to say, "Surely you are not going to ask for a party again?"

While he munched on his cereal, Bijoy rolled his eyes, as if to ask "Why not?"

It seemed as though they were communicating through TELEPATHY—a way of communicating your thoughts or feelings to someone else without using speech or writing. SIBLINGS often share such special bonds as to be able to 'talk' like this.

Having finished his breakfast, Bijoy got up from his chair. *There was a time when the full house would be ringing with music and parties,* he thought.

He had always had a soft spot for this time of the year. It is so jam-packed with festivals! After Christmas, there is the New Year and then, in January, the BHOGALI BIHU festival is celebrated across Assam. But this year, everything seemed so dull.

Truth be told, Bijoy did not actually want a big Christmas party. All he wanted was to spend some time with his family. He looked sadly at them as he walked out of the room.

The disappointment

My parents are always, always busy working from home, thought Bijoy. *Physically, they are at home, but their minds are always in their office. My sister is also always glued to her phone, either attending online classes or CHATTING with her friends.*

The only thing that Bijoy had been looking forward to for Christmas was a visit from Prasant mama, his uncle who lived abroad. He visited them on Christmas every year. "But alas! This time, he is not coming," moaned Bijoy.

Also, shortly after Christmas, every New Year, Bijoy and his family visited his grandparents. Koka and Aita (as they lovingly called them in Assamese) lived in their **ANCESTRAL** house in a small village nestled among the lush tea gardens of Assam. This time, however, all such plans had to be called off. "It is too risky to travel in this pandemic," Ma and Papa had said.

Bijoy **MISSED** his grandparents terribly now. It had been quite a long time since he last saw them. They could not even meet virtually because Koka and Aita did not know how to use a **SMARTPHONE**.

So, a disappointed Bijoy retired to his bedroom. He did not come out until his sister knocked on his door later that day.

Surprise!

And what a surprise it was! He had got parcels! "Christmas gifts from Koka and Aita? Wow!" exclaimed Bijoy.

Aita had knitted two beautiful **SWEATERS** for him and his sister, and Koka had sent them storybooks! Bijoy would not have been so happy even if Santa Claus had actually come and gifted him presents.

Bijoy immediately called his grandparents. It was such a delight to talk to them. Prasant mama also video-called and wished them a Merry Christmas.

So much the better, Bijoy's parents had made a very special lunch too: mouth-watering rohu masor tenga (tangy rohu fish curry), delicious duck curry with ash gourd and dhekia bhaji (stir-fried fiddlehead ferns) served with rice and daal. Mamta had also made him a Christmas CAKE

"I baked it all by myself!" said Mamta.

"I don't believe you," Bijoy teased. And the rest of the afternoon was spent in merrymaking. Bijoy could not have been happier.

So, looking back now, as he ate Mamta's cake, Bijoy realized that this year's Christmas was not so bad, after all. "It is, in fact, one of the best Christmas CELEBRATIONS I have ever had!" he beamed

Memory

World Heritage Day is celebrated on April 18. A class has come to visit the group of monuments at Mahabalipuram one of the world heritage sites in Tamil Nadu. Observe the picture and answer the questions given below.

Q1. What is the name of the monument?

Q2. What are the two students sitting on the rocks doing?

Q3. How many students are standing along with their teacher?

Q4. What is the tourist guide pointing at?

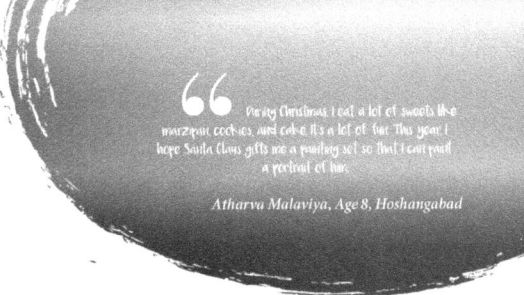

Unity in Diversity

By Siddhesh Bhusane

Today in class, Vanshika listened to her teacher talk about unity in diversity in India. She said, "There are many great differences or diversities in our country, like those of LANGUAGE, dress, food, religion and many more things."

The teacher continued, "As a part of this, make a project on the DIVERSITY of language in India. The best project will be awarded a prize."

Tricky project

Vanshika was excited to do the project, but she did not know much about the languages of India. She was wondering how to go about it. She knew that she had to research in the library and the internet but she wanted to ask someone about it.

Then suddenly, she remembered that her sister Vidya was a linguist—a person knowing many languages. She would be able to help her! Vanshika did her work on the project and went to her sister's room.

At the door, Vanshika said, "Didi, may I come in? I need your help."

Vidya was doing her school home work, but kept it aside and asked her sister to come in.

Vanshika asked her sister, "Didi, I have to do a project on language for school. Could you tell me about the various languages spoken in our country?"

Vidya said, "In our country, many different languages are spoken. Marathi and Gujarati are spoken in Maharashtra, Gujarat, Goa, Dadra, Nagar Haveli, Daman and Diu. ASSAMESE is used in Assam and Arunachal Pradesh while BENGALI is spoken in West Bengal, Tripura, parts of Assam, Jharkhand, Bihar, Andaman and Nicobar Islands. In Jammu and Kashmir Dogri is spoken. Hindi is the language that most people converse in Bihar, Uttar Pradesh, Delhi, Madhya Pradesh, Chhattisgarh, Himachal Pradesh, Haryana and Rajasthan."

Vidya continued, "Besides these languages, there are many more languages. Kannada is spoken in Karnataka; Kashmiri in Jammu and Kashmir; Konkani in Goa, parts of Maharashtra and Karnataka; Hindi, along with Bhojpuri and Maithili, is spoken in different parts of Bihar; Malayalam in Kerala; Nepali in Sikkim and northern parts of West Bengal;

Oriya in Odisha; Sanskrit in Uttarakhand; **SANTHALI** in Chhotanagpur; Tamil in Tamil Nadu and Pondicherry; **TELEGU** in Telangana, Andhra Pradesh and parts of Odisha and Karnataka; Urdu in Jammu and Kashmir, Telangana, Delhi, Bihar, Uttar Pradesh and Jharkhand."

United we stand, divided we fall

"Oh God, so many languages in one country!" Vanshika exclaimed.

Vidya said, "But in spite of so many languages, there is **UNITY** in India. Lots of people go from one city to another or even from one state to another in search of a job or an education. These people take their own language with them, but also adapt to the language of the state that they are in."

"But Didi, English also is known by many people across the country," Vanshika said.

Vidya said, "That is true. But it is not an Indian language. We adopted it when India was ruled by the British. These days, English is used in offices, schools, colleges and courts in India."

"With so many different languages, how come there is still unity in our country?" asked Vanshika.

"This is because many states have adopted the languages of other states. Every language is a medium of **communication**. A language is necessary to converse with one another. You will not believe this, but most animals and birds talk among themselves using their own language."

Vanshika thanked her sister and prepared her project based on the information. She realized that, like in India, where we speak different languages but are one united nation, so is the case for the world where we speak many languages, but are united as people. As much as languages are different, people are the same. We need to look for things that **bind** us rather than divide us.

The Maker of Modern India

By Kumud Kumar

We live in a modern, independent India and Raja Ram Mohan Roy was the first person who laid the foundation of this modern nation.

Ram Mohan was born on May 22, 1772, in the Hooghly district of Bengal. His father, Ramakant Roy, was a wealthy landlord and his mother, Tarini Devi, was a religious woman.

At that time, people in India practised the **PURDAH SYSTEM** where women had to cover themselves from head to toe or be hidden behind high walls and curtains outdoors and even inside their homes; **Suti**—a practice where widows had to jump in the funeral pyre of their dead husbands; child marriage where children below the age of 18 were married; and newborn female babies were killed. These social evils were practised throughout the country.

Many people in the country were not educated and women had to do what they were told.

A life-changing decision

Ram Mohan Roy was first married when he was 9 years old. His first wife passed away at a very young age and soon his second marriage was held at the age of 10. He had two sons—Radhaprasad and Ramaprasad.

At the age of 14, he wanted to become a monk. But his mother opposed his decision.

After that, he travelled to Patna to study ARABIC and Persian languages.

In Varanasi (then Kashi), he learned Sanskrit and studied the Vedas and the Upanishads. The **VEDAS** taught him that idol worship is unnecessary as God doesn't have a body and is pure and cannot be created by man. He learned to believe in the truth and nothing else.

These lessons had a great **impact** on Ram Mohan and he began to question idol worship and several religious rituals.

This led to a life-changing incident in his life. His father was a devoted idol worshipper while Ram Mohan wasn't. One day, a debate broke out between him and his father about IDOL worship.

Ram Mohan said, "Father, why do you worship idols? You should only believe in god. The idols are created by man and WORSHIPPING them is meaningless!"

His father was deeply offended and said, "Where did you learn such nonsense? Idol worship is a means to reach God."

"Father, why not worship him directly?" asked Ram Mohan.

After that argument, Ram Mohan left his house.

In 1803, when his father passed away, he began opposing idol worship and rituals openly.

He supported the worship of one God as described in the Vedas.

In 1805, he met John Digby, a British officer who taught him English. This helped him understand the lifestyle and practices of people in English-speaking countries.

A fight for safety and equality

From 1809 to 1814, Ram Mohan lived in Rangpur city (now in Bangladesh). While earning for his family, he met people of all religions. He understood that to fight social evils, he would not get any support from society. So, he kept increasing his knowledge and experiences.

In 1814, Ram Mohan moved to Kolkata. In 1815, he founded the Atmiya Sabha—an organisation that invited people to share their IDEAS.

In 1817, he founded the Hindu College in Kolkata to promote modern education and English language. He wanted the number of literate people to increase as only then would they question the society and its evil practices. He believed that educated people will think RATIONALLY.

Ram Mohan's work for modernising the society was not welcomed by many and he had to face several challenges but he never lost COURAGE and kept fighting and spreading awareness.

To reach the masses with his teachings, in 1821, he launched a Bengali newspaper Samvad Kaumudi and a Persian newspaper Mirat-ul-Akhbar in 1822.

In these newspapers, he wrote about Sati, child marriage, purdah system and idol worship. His writings made people think about reforming the society.

They were forced to think:

"Why do we get children married when they are supposed to play at that age?"

"Why do we burn women alive on the funeral pyre?"

"What is the need for keeping women behind the purdah and separating them in society?"

"Why can't we let widows have a new life by getting them remarried?"

This marked the beginning of a **reformed** society.

Sowing the seeds of change

In 1828, he founded the Brahmo Samaj and continued to fight for various social reforms through this organisation.

His biggest success was the *ABOLITION* of Sati. The practice of burning the wife alive on the husband's funeral pyre. It was a terrible practice where the woman was FORCIBLY burned.

Ram Mohan took the battle of Sati from India to England. Due to his efforts, the British government banned Sati on December 4, 1829.

In 1831, the Mughal Emperor Akbar II gave the title of 'Raja' to Ram Mohan Roy.

He died on September 27, 1833, in Bristol, England. In his honour, the British government named a PEDESTRIAN path in Bristol as 'Raja Ram Mohan Walk'.

Rabindranath Tagore, a famous poet, described him as the Father and Maker of Modern India

Answers to puzzles

Page 61: Solve It

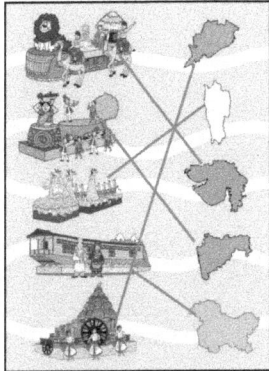

Page 99: Sequence

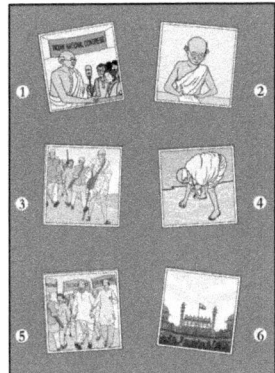

Page 73: Word Search

A	I	M	D	U	A	H	A	P	M	J	Z	S	O	W	V
S	O	T	E	F	A	D	E	P	O	L	Q	U	Q	P	X
A	J	M	A	S	W	A	R	A	J	K	F	D	Z	S	F
L	G	I	D	R	E	S	O	E	K	R	K	I	S	K	R
P	A	D	A	D	E	A	H	S	L	C	C	N	U	A	E
D	T	N	A	L	S	I	M	O	N	B	Y	D	R	V	E
I	N	I	O	E	F	U	L	D	O	W	H	I	K	M	D
A	R	G	J	P	A	T	F	E	R	R	B	A	T	X	O
N	O	H	D	E	N	E	P	N	T	K	W	N	V	Y	M
H	T	T	R	U	T	H	Q	Y	H	A	G	P	L	Z	H
B	I	M	S	O	K	N	P	L	S	M	Z	R	O	J	N

Page 122: Odd One Out

Page 227: Find The Gifts

Page 131: Solve It

A - 5   D - 2
B - 3   E - 1
C - 4

Page 184: Solve It

A-3, B-5,
C-2, D-4, E-5

Page 238: Decode
She gets a chocolate float.